SKELMERSDALE

FICTION RESERVE STOCK LL60

AUTHOR	CLASS
OLIVER, B	A FC

TITLE The London maker

Lancashire County Library

3011 8000 01770

D1349850

THE LONDON MAKER

1

A thin misty early morning drizzle cast a halo round the lighted street lamp shining in the gloom outside 93 Woodlands Park Road, Fulham.

'I hate these November mornings,' said postman Jim Barnes to himself as he pushed a letter through the box at number 93. 'Damp but not yet cold, and my bones are aching. Retirement can't come too soon.' He tramped on to his next delivery, avoiding the puddles in the uneven pavement, and musing on what he would do as a pensioner.

On the other side of the front door, Daphne Fleet picked up the letter. Unlike Jim, she still had a long way to go before retirement from her job at the Foreign Office, and looked forward each day to receiving the post just before she had to set out for the office. She lived with her ageing mother, and the post had become something of an event in a life that was increasingly bereft of significant events. However, the letter that had been delivered on this murky November morning was to prove an event which would bring about a dramatic change in her daily routine. Addressed to her, it was written by a firm of solicitors in Cruff, Scotland, a firm of whom she had never heard. It read:

20 High Street
Cruff
East Lothian
Scotland
20 November 1996.

Dear Miss Fleet,

We very much regret to inform you of the death last month of your aunt, Mrs Mildred Fletcher. We apologise for not letting you or your mother know about the funeral which took place locally, but we were not able to locate your address in time.

We are the sole executors of your late aunt's will. In the will, your aunt has bequeathed you her antique bracket clock in fond memory of the days when she taught you to tell the time using this clock.

We can arrange to have the clock delivered to you, or, if you would prefer, given the somewhat delicate nature of the item, we will hold it for you to collect at your convenience. Please let us know which alternative would suit you.

Yours sincerely
Smith and Drury,
Solicitors and commissioners of oath

The actual signature above the typed names at the foot of the letter was so indecipherable that it could have been either Smith or Drury or almost any name in the telephone directory.

Daphne went upstairs to show the letter to her mother.

'I think it must be thirty years since I last saw my sister Mildred,' her mother informed her. 'We lost contact with her after Daddy died and we moved here. I am sorry to learn that she has died, but we never got on all that well together after

2

she got married, although I can remember taking you up to Scotland in the summer holidays for several years running when you were a young girl. She had a cottage on the outskirts of a village. Beautiful place in the summer, but I'm not sure that I would like to live there at this time of the year. I can remember you used to play with her son Andrew. He was a year or two older than you. I wonder what has happened to him?'

Daphne thought about the letter on her way to the office. The thin drizzle running down the windows of the bus depressed her. 'Can Scotland be any worse?' she thought. On the spur of the moment she decided to go to Scotland and collect the clock herself. One of the advantages of working in the civil service was the generous leave granted to those with the length of service that Daphne had accumulated. She still had more than two weeks due to her this year that she had not been able to make up her mind how to use. As soon as she arrived at the office that Thursday she successfully applied to have the following week off, and contacted Smith and Drury to let them know she would be coming to collect the clock the following Monday.

On her return home in the evening she told her mother what she intended to do, and suggested she might like to keep her company on the journey. She had recently bought a red MG two-seater sports car, and she thought the long journey to Scotland would test its mettle as well as hers as a driver. But, as Daphne guessed only too well, the idea of a day being driven at seventy or more miles an hour was not an appealing one to her mother, who preferred her creature comforts to the spartan attractions of a long fast drive in the MG.

Daphne used the following Saturday morning to gather together and pack as many items of warm clothing as she thought she might need for a few days in Scotland, and then part of the afternoon rejecting the larger ones as she tried to get everything in the limited amount of luggage space available in the small car. 'Just as well mother didn't come,' she thought, 'we would have had to rope a wardrobe on the roof.'

The drizzle was still falling when she set off at first light on Sunday morning. Daphne was a competent driver and the MG did its stuff eating up the miles without any problems. The traffic was minimal and the MG had no difficulty over-taking the relatively few slower moving vehicles on the road on a November Sunday.

By the time she reached the Scottish border the drizzle had turned to snow, and she was quite pleased to find a room in the only hotel in the village when she finally reached Cruff at the end of a long day's drive.

The following morning she presented herself at the offices of Messrs Smith and Drury. She was ushered into the room of a Mr John Sergeant, a large and somewhat forbidding look-ing young man with glasses and a very precise Scottish accent. Daphne showed him the letter she had received by way of introduction and, after offering his commiserations on her aunt's death in his resonant Scottish voice, he pro-duced the clock and stood it on his desk.

Daphne looked at it. It was a neat clock with a round silver face and a case made of a dark mahogany-coloured wood.

'It seems to work,' Mr Sergeant told her, 'and it strikes the quarters on a gong. We've stuffed some soft paper inside to stop the gong making too much noise … I hope that is satis-factory?' noticing the disconcerted look on Daphne's face.

Daphne was indeed perturbed. Of one thing she was very nearly certain. This could not be the clock on which her aunt had taught her how to tell the time. It might have been thirty or more years ago, but she had spent a lot of time looking at the clock then and her aunt had been very proud of it, telling her that it was by a London maker. This one had a name on the dial which was very German sounding. Also Daphne remembered her aunt's clock had played a tune on bells while this one had a gong.

'Was this the only clock that my aunt had?' enquired Daphne.

'I think so,' replied the solicitor, 'the other contents of the cottage have been sold by auction and the cottage itself is up for sale, but I do have somewhere here a catalogue of the contents. Ah yes, here it is ... there were not many items worth auctioning. No, there was not another clock.'

Daphne was convinced that this was not the same clock, but felt that there was very little she could do about it. She decided not to convey her misgivings to Mr Sergeant.

'I've decided to spend a day or two here now that I've come all this way,' she told him. 'Perhaps I could collect the clock first thing on Wednesday morning before I go back, if that is convenient?'

The solicitor nodded his consent.

'By the way, I presume my cousin Andrew was mentioned in the will, assuming he is still alive?'

'Yes indeed, Miss Fleet, your cousin was the only other beneficiary, and he inherits the rest of the estate.'

'Does he live round here?'

'No,' replied the solicitor rather unhelpfully, 'he lives abroad.'

'I suppose you must have some way of contacting him. Perhaps you would tell me how I can get in touch with him – I haven't seen him for years.'

'Well, we know that he is a man who travels extensively in his job. We have already paid out in respect of the contents and the cash part of the estate when he was staying for a while in his mother's cottage, but following the payment we know that he went abroad again. I can give you the forwarding address he left – ah yes, here it is – a holiday address, but I understand he intends staying there for a few weeks.' He wrote out the address which turned out to be in a town called Sliema in Malta.

'Well, thank you, Mr Sergeant. I will see you again on

Wednesday. Can you suggest what I should see here in Cruff, or is there anything you can especially recommend to do?'

Mr Sergeant looked her up and down. 'There's the church,' he said in his clipped Scottish accent, managing to sound the 'r' in church. 'And you can always go for a walk across the hills. Some of the best walking country in the world.' Again he sounded the 'r' in world.

Daphne was beginning to regret her decision to come to Scotland, especially when she was met by a flurry of snow as she stepped outside the solicitor's office. She prided herself on her fitness, the result of twice-weekly badminton sessions, but shivered in the cold morning air. She looked in the shop windows, choosing a street with smaller specialised shops, rather than seeking out the local supermarket which she suspected might not compare with what was available in that epitome of current fashion and design, Fulham. Looking idly in the windows but not stopping long at any one because of the cold, she suddenly froze, this time not from the cold. She was outside a shop with a simple sign Cruff Antiques, and there, occupying pride of place in the heavily barred window was a clock, a bracket clock. Daphne stared at it. It had a familiar look about it, with a brass dial and a handsome wooden case.

She found herself pushing open the door which caused a small bell to tinkle. This produced from a back room a smart-looking mature lady dressed in warm Scottish tweeds. Daphne asked if she could look around, not wishing to draw attention to the clock. But the lady in the shop was well used to this approach by customers and soon noticed Daphne's interest in the clock.

'It's an eighteenth-century, triple fusée, musical bracket clock in a walnut case. It plays several tunes including a Scottish one,' she told her. As she spoke, she reached over to the clock, opened the front bezel and moved the minute hand up to the next hour. There was a click of metal on metal

6

and the clock struck the hour on a high-pitched bell. Then it began to play a tune. With a thrill, Daphne realised that a chord was equally stirring at the back of her mind – vaguely she recognised the tinkling music being struck out on the clock's ancient bells. Although it was a long time ago now, she had heard the tune so many times when she was at an impressionable age that she felt sure that this was the same music she had listened to in her aunt's cottage all those years ago.

The tweedy shopkeeper was talking again. 'I can't tell you what the tune is, I'm afraid. I'm not very musical and I couldn't recognise the latest top of the pops, let alone something dating back to the eighteenth century. But whatever it is, it's quite catchy in its own way, and I find myself humming the tune quite unconsciously.' Daphne agreed.

'The maker, George Clark of London, was working approximately between 1725 and 1750. I have looked up his name in a book of clockmakers. It seems he was quite famous in his time and was a member of the Clockmakers' Company of London.'

'It's not a local clock, then?' Daphne asked.

'Well, it wasn't made here in Scotland, of course, but I did buy it locally. It was part of a deceased's estate and I was lucky to get it. I had to go down on bended knees to my bank manager in order to be able to find the wherewithal.' Daphne looked at the antique dealer in her respectable tweeds and found it difficult to accept the picture which this statement conjured up. She turned over the label attached to the clock, and let out a gasp when she saw the price on it – £25,000.

'It's a wonderful clock, and I should love to own it, but I don't think I have the right technique with bank managers,' she told the knowledgeable antique dealer. 'Can you tell me anything more about where it came from?'

'I am afraid I cannot tell you from whom I bought it, beyond saying it was obtained privately.'

7

Realising that she was unlikely to find out anything more, Daphne thanked the dealer and made her way out of the antique shop more than ever convinced that the clock in the window had belonged to her aunt and should now rightfully belong to her. She resolved to collect the clock that the solicitor said was hers that morning, and then consider what action to take. Since there seemed little else to do on a snowy day in Cruff she retraced her steps, told the solicitor she had changed her mind about staying in the village and picked up the clock there and then.

'By the way, how long ago was it that my cousin went to Malta?' she asked.

'Only last week,' replied the solicitor. 'After we made the first payment out of the estate.'

'Did you know him well?'

'Not really. He didn't live round here. The firm drew up your aunt's will many years ago, but that's about all we had to do with the family as far as I know.' Daphne thanked him, took up the clock in the bag she had brought for the purpose, and left to return to her hotel room.

She ordered a cup of coffee and considered her position. Clearly the two clocks had been switched. Her cousin must have known how valuable his mother's bracket clock was, and substituted a cheaper one in the belief that Daphne would never remember what it looked like after such a long lapse of time. What to do now? Simply go back home and be satisfied to have received something which had cost her nothing more than a trip to Scotland? She looked at the clock she had been given and guessed that its value would be hardly much more than the expenses she had incurred in obtaining it.

She thought again about her cousin Andrew. She could remember almost nothing about him, and felt she would almost certainly not recognise him after all these years. What kind of man was he that would stoop so low?

She took out the address that the solicitor had provided

8

and read it again. Malta! The snow was blowing against the hotel windows and the wind whining through the crack in the ill-fitting door. She found herself making another spur-of-the-moment decision, something that was contrary to her normal pattern of behaviour at the Foreign Office where a decision was reached only after long and profound consideration. She would go to Malta, seek out Andrew and see what he had to say for himself. She still had the two or three weeks left of her annual leave and few commitments in London other than a responsibility to her widowed mother.

She was of a practical nature, a disposition which had helped her career at the Foreign Office, but had perhaps explained why she was still single, as she had never been able to find a man with whom she felt she could manage her life as well as she could by herself. Thus resolved, she packed her bags, settled the hotel bill, phoned her mother to let her know she was returning straight away, and made the long journey back to London without incident.

The next morning, back in London, she described events in Scotland to her mother, who could throw little light on either her cousin, her late aunt or the clock. She booked an air ticket for Malta for the next day.

2

By midday on Wednesday she was stepping out of the plane in Malta to a warm but windy day. She found a taxi and got the driver to take her to a reasonable hotel in Sliema. The journey took her through a maze of densely crowded streets teeming with people and traffic. 'Too many Maltese and not enough Malta,' she thought as the taxi snarled up in another jam. The whole place had a faintly oriental atmosphere. Sliema turned out to be a suburb of the capital Valetta, with an extensive frontage to both the sea and to one of the creeks making up the Grand Harbour complex. A vast armada of yachts bobbed up and down in the sluggish water, many of them looking permanent features of the seascape. Across the water were the imposing walls of the old fortifications built four centuries ago.

Once ensconced in the hotel, she found out from the receptionist that the address Andrew was staying at was only a short walk away. She had been trying to decide what her plan of campaign should be when she met him. It looked as if her cousin was something of a scoundrel who had gone abroad very smartly after cashing in what should have been her inheritance, although she could see that he might be a bit peeved to have found out that his mother's most valued possession had been willed to someone he scarcely knew. She had some experience in negotiating at the Foreign Office,

10

and decided that as right was on her side, she would take a tough stance. But she was little prepared for what met her at the address at St John's Road, Sliema. The house was terraced and built of the same limestone blocks as almost every other house in the district. In addition to a number the house had a name: Veronica.

Her knock at the door was answered by a short, dark, stout woman and an equally short, dark, stout man. Daphne,who was in build and colour the exact opposite of the two Maltese, found herself looking down on them.

'I am looking for a Mr Andrew Fletcher...'

At the mention of his name the couple became extremely excited, gesticulating and shouting in both English and an unintelligible Maltese. Eventually when they had calmed down they invited Daphne inside their home.

'We too are looking for Mr Andrew Fletcher,' they informed her. They then went on to tell her that Andrew had come to stay with them at the invitation of their daughter, Veronica, who had met Andrew when he had come on holiday to the island in the summer. Andrew was a keen sailor and had taken their daughter out sailing each day. But yesterday the couple had not returned at the end of their day's sailing as they usually had. The family were strict Catholics and seemed more concerned that Andrew had departed to another harbour in Malta with their daughter, who was, they said, aged only twenty-eight, and, it seemed, a virgin, rather than that the couple might have come to grief at sea. At this very moment their son was making enquiries around the harbour.

The picture that was emerging of Andrew was increasingly unfavourable. The catalogue of his misdemeanours was lengthening.

While they were exchanging information, a young man came in and was introduced as their son, Mark. Taller than his parents, he was a likeable-looking young man, who Daphne guessed, was younger than his sister. He said in very

11

good English, 'I have found out who hired the boat to Veronica and Andrew. His name is Feranc Borg and his boat is quite a large one with a powerful engine. His brother lives down the road and I have arranged to go and see him now to find out if he can tell me where the boat might be, or, where Veronica is.'

'I should like to come with you, if I may,' said Daphne. 'I have a very keen interest in finding my cousin.'

So the two of them made their way the short distance to another house built in the same style of limestone blocks. They were met at the doorway by a middle-aged man with a bald head and a strong smell of garlic. He too, like most Maltese, spoke fluent English.

'Yes, that's right,' he said, 'my brother has been hiring out his boat to an Englishman and a Maltese girl. They have visited all the harbours in Malta these last few days, so yesterday my brother suggested that they should go over to Sicily. They both seemed very keen on this suggestion and arrived with plenty of luggage and off they went.'

Mark was visibly upset by this news. His sister had gone off abroad with an Englishman and the family honour was clearly at stake.

'How far is it to Sicily?' Daphne enquired.

'About ninety miles – they will be there in only a few hours. My brother's boat is a seagoing vessel and he is used to the trip.'

'Just a minute,' interrupted Daphne, 'who was driving this boat?'

'My brother, of course. He goes with the hire of the boat. He knows all the harbours of Malta like the back of his hand, and often goes over to Italy.'

Well, thought Daphne, at least the honour of Veronica's family should be less at stake if Andrew was not alone with her on the boat. But she was still some way from catching up with her wandering cousin.

'When were they expected back?' Daphne asked.

'Ah,' said the boat-owner's brother, 'while my brother will of course be coming back, I don't know that his passengers will be returning with him.'

This piece of information alarmed Mark even more. 'I must go to Sicily. I have to find out what is happening. Veronica must come back.' Poor Veronica, thought Daphne. Women's lib. still has some way to go in this part of the world.

An animated discussion of the situation followed, during which it emerged that their host had a similar vessel to that of his brother and that it was available for hire. However Mark's enthusiasm to protect the family name waned somewhat when he discovered the cost of hiring the vessel and its owner. Once again Daphne found herself making a spur-of-the-moment decision.

'Look,' she said, 'I can easily get some cash on my credit cards. I will finance this expedition to Sicily if you will take me with you. I have a very good reason for wanting to find my cousin. But you must give us a fair price on the boat hire.' Mark nodded agreement. The boat-owner seemed to delight in the protracted negotiations involved in establishing a fair price, pointing out the difficulty of knowing when the return journey would be. Finally a fee was arranged and it was agreed that all three would depart as soon as possible the next day.

The following morning found Daphne at the quayside dressed in her trouser suit and trainers and armed with an overnight bag. The wind was quite stiff but the boat-owner seemed sanguine enough. Daphne watched with fascination as the boat threaded its way out of the magnificent harbour with its ancient fortifications towering over them.

'If you would like to make yourself comfortable below you might be happier – we are about to hit the open sea,' the boat-owner suggested to Daphne. Not being the best of sailors, she took his advice. She stretched out on one of the bunks and was musing what to say to Andrew when she finally confronted him, when Mark came down to join her in the cabin. She was somewhat irritated when he started to engage her in puerile conversation, but irritation gave way to alarm when he moved closer to her and placed his arm round her shoulder. She soon discovered that whatever moral restrictions applied to his sister did not apply to him. Daphne had spent several years in Rome during her Foreign Office career and was well experienced at dealing with the amorous advances of the Italian male, but had to admit that to judge from her current partner the Maltese had little to learn from the Italians. The fact that she was at least fifteen years his senior seemed to be of no consequence to him, but she did manage to bring home to him that they were both on the trip to settle family differences, not to create further problems. Finally Mark returned on deck with the boat-owner, leaving Daphne to her thoughts.

She was aroused from her reveries later by the two men calling out that they were coming into the port of Syracuse in Sicily. Regular ferries plied between Syracuse and Valetta in Malta, and the Maltese boat-owner told her that this was where his brother always went on his quite frequent trips, so he was confident that he would find his brother there. This confidence was justified when he excitedly pointed out a vessel very similar to the one they were in, moored by itself at a jetty in the harbour. 'That's it. I shall have to clear customs and do my paper work,' he told them as he tied up next to his brother's boat. 'There's a policeman there. You can see if he knows where the three of them are.'

Mark spoke fluent Italian, while Daphne was familiar with the language having spent several years in Rome. They went up to the policeman and asked if he knew where the sailors from the nearby vessel might be, not expecting a positive reply. They were therefore surprised that he did indeed know – they were in the local prison.

'Why on earth are they in prison?' asked Daphne.

'I can't tell you,' said the policeman. 'You had best go to the police station yourselves to find out.' He gave them instructions on how to get there and they set off through the narrow Sicilian streets.

At the police station they were lucky to find a senior official who was prepared to talk to them.

'Yes, it's true, we have arrested three people on the boat you mention, two Maltese and an Englishman. It was one of my men who was guarding the boat. We have suspected for some time that it was involved in smuggling, so we checked it out when it tied up this time. We found contraband goods on board, which we have confiscated. We are considering what action to take against those on board.'

Mark was visibly shaken by this unexpected turn of events. 'What contraband was it?' he asked.

'I am afraid I cannot tell you that,' the police officer replied.

'The woman is my sister and I can't believe that she would be involved in smuggling. She has lived at home with us all her life and I am sure the family would have known if something was going on,' he said naively.

And Daphne was surprised that Andrew was involved, although each fresh piece of information she learned about him seemed to blacken his character further.

'However,' said the Sicilian policeman, 'when we checked the Englishman's passport we found that it had been stamped for entry into Malta quite recently, while we know that this boat has been making regular visits here for some time. We therefore released him.'

As a Foreign Office official Daphne noted that her passport had been stamped on her arrival in Malta and guessed that this was regular practice for a country which was not a member of the European Community. What a lucky break for Andrew! The devil looks after his own, she thought.

'Can I see my sister?' Mark asked.

'Yes,' said the police official, 'and you can give her this letter that the Englishman left for her. I would tell you at this stage it seems unlikely that we will press charges against her, and that if you can wait a while we may have some good news for you as soon as we have completed our investigations.' The police officer seemed quite sympathetic.

Daphne and Mark were led to the meagre cell where his sister Veronica was held. There was a compassionate reconciliation following which Mark introduced Daphne and then gave his sister the reasonably comforting news passed on to him by the police officer. Veronica then read the letter left by Andrew. As she read it, she began crying, finally thrusting it over to Daphne and Mark. 'Dear Veronica,' it read,

You will know me well enough by now not to be surprised by my sudden change of plan. I have been released. The police officer has told me that they are unlikely to keep you here for long, and that you will soon be released too.

I have very much enjoyed my stay with you in Malta, and hope that you also had an enjoyable time. As you know, I intended to return to Rome after our visit to Sicily, in a few days' time. But this stay by myself in a police cell has perhaps sobered me up after being intoxicated by your lively personality. It has served to break the magic of our holiday together and caused me to think again what we were proposing to do. I know your family will not have approved of me as soon as they knew we had gone off together. For my part I am a restless soul and it would be wrong of me to pursue our relationship further in the knowledge that eventually it would not lead to the sort of long-term commitment that you and your family would expect.

Therefore I am leaving, although not without a great deal of remorseful feelings. I believe it might be too

16

upsetting for you to tell you this in person, and I sincerely hope you will think that what I am doing is for the best. I wish you every success and will always remember my stay in Malta,

All my love,

Andrew

'What a rotter,' declared Daphne. Mark's comments were all in Maltese, but sounded considerably more forceful than Daphne's statement.

So as soon as he was freed Andrew had skipped off leaving Veronica in jail, and had not had the guts to tell her to her face! Daphne's opinion of her cousin, already low, went down another notch.

Veronica calmed down after considerable comforting by Daphne and Mark, who pointed out that at least she had enjoyed a holiday without having actually lost anything, although Mark was acting and talking about Andrew as if he had taken Veronica's most precious asset. The situation shortly improved when the Sicilian police inspector came in to tell Veronica that he was satisfied that she had no part in the smuggling and that the police were proceeding against Borg the boat owner whom they had long suspected. Veronica was therefore free to go. The inspector took her back upstairs where she was given the two cases of hers that the police had been holding.

Daphne, Veronica and Mark decided that they had best now return to Malta – at least they had secured a fifty per cent success in their mission. But it looked as if Andrew's trail was likely to go cold. Would he now be here in Syracuse or wandering about Sicily? As an afterthought Daphne asked the police officer if he knew where Andrew had gone.

'Well, I do not know positively where he might be, but we did take from him an address when he left. It is in Rome, but it is confidential and I am not permitted to give it to you.'

Daphne thought hard. 'I suspect that Mr Fletcher has committed a crime in Scotland and I am offering a reward to anyone who can provide information which may lead to bringing him to justice,' she told the Sicilian police inspector in her best Foreign Office manner, without departing from the truth.

'How much might that reward be?' enquired the policeman tentatively.

Looking round at the rather rundown police station she guessed at a figure which might be appropriate in the circumstances, bearing in mind the funds she had available.

'£100, or 275,000 lire,' she said.

The policeman thought for a moment. 'And how and when will this reward be paid?' he enquired.

'In cash, as soon as I get the address,' she told him bluntly. The police inspector went to his office and returned with a piece of paper which he gave to Daphne without comment. On it was written an address in Rome.

'Thank you,' Daphne said, handing the policeman the money. 'I shall not require a receipt.'

The three of them left the police station with Mark carrying Veronica's cases, and headed back to the jetty where they had left the second Borg brother. 'We've got a surprise for him,' Mark observed. However, when they reached the jetty it was they who were in for a shock. Neither Borg nor his boat were anywhere to be seen. The same policeman they had spoken to originally was still standing guard over the first Borg brother's boat. They asked him if he knew anything. He pointed laconically to a distant vessel disappearing out of the harbour. It would seem that Mr Borg No. Two, on learning what had happened to his brother, had no wish to share his fate, let alone do anything about his release from prison.

Daphne again thanked her Foreign Office training in that she had paid only half the agreed fee on the way out, holding back the balance for the return. Clearly the boatman must have had a guilty conscience to have preferred an immediate return home and a sacrifice of his fee to honouring his commitment to Mark and Veronica.

'There is a ferry to Malta,' Mark told Daphne.

'Let's see if we can catch it then,' Daphne replied. 'It probably won't be any more expensive than our hired boat, and I will pay the fares.'

Not long after, all three were installed in the speeding ferry. Daphne figured she had an obligation to go back to Malta with Mark and Veronica, and in any case she needed to pick up her bags from the hotel. Already she had resolved to go to Rome, a city she knew and loved very well, to see if she could pick up Andrew's trail again. The repeated set-backs she had so far suffered had served to strengthen her resolve to catch up with her wayward cousin.

The steady rocking motion of the ferry soon had Mark nodding off to sleep, but Daphne, who had taken it easy on the way over, was now wide awake, as was Veronica. After a couple of glasses of sweet Maltese wine, Veronica became much more composed, and began telling her story to Daphne. It seemed that she was far from being the domesticated flower that the other members of the family had made her out to be. Indeed, she had a good job as a multilingual receptionist at a four-star hotel, bringing home good money. Her brother, by contrast, was less diligent, got only casual jobs, and was rather looked down on by Veronica. It was Veronica who kept the family going financially, which was why they were concerned not to lose her. Moreover, it became clear as Veronica started on her third glass of wine, that Andrew was by no means the first person with whom she had had an intimate relationship. Her position as receptionist at a first-class hotel brought her into contact with a steady stream of personable men. Veronica was quite happy to have someone different to recount her various adventures to, and as they neared Malta, Daphne felt that far from rescuing an

19

innocent maiden in distress, she had encountered something of a modern young lady who listened with interest to Daphne's own recent adventures. Daphne's first impression of Veronica was clearly way out.

Later, when they had all reached Sliema, they exchanged addresses and made their farewells. Daphne returned to her hotel, and managed to get the reception staff to book her on a plane to Rome within the week. She was thankful the credit card companies had been so generous in repeatedly offering her ever larger credit limits. It certainly looked as if she would be needing them on this trip. That night she slept soundly after her exhausting but exhilarating adventure in Sicily.

3

On her arrival in Rome, Daphne booked into a small hotel that she remembered from her Foreign Office days. After unpacking her bags, she set off to find the address the Sicilian policeman had given her, hoping that it would not turn out to be a wild goose chase, as she had little hope of picking up Andrew's trail if the address proved false. The taxi drive there proved to be an exciting contrast to the usual daily journey she made in London, and different too from the drives in Malta when she was never sure which side of the road they were supposed to be on. The noise of the vehicles, particularly the aggressive use of their horns, and the frequent shouted conversations with other road-users, seemed overwhelming. After a mercifully short ride the taxi drew up outside a large terraced block now used as guest houses, although with the air of once being a building of some style. Daphne paid off the taxi, climbed the two or three stone steps that led to a very imposing but rather derelict door that stood wide open.

Once inside, she encountered a rather benign-looking middle-aged lady with a kindly weather-beaten face who turned out to be in charge of the building. Summoning up her best Italian, Daphne enquired whether a Mr Andrew Fletcher lived there. Much to Daphne's relief the concierge said that he did. However he was not at home at present, having gone off on 'one of his trips'.

21

'Does he often go off like that?' enquired Daphne.

'Oh yes,' replied the good lady, 'usually for weeks at a time.'

'How long has he been living here?'

'For about three years now. He is a good tenant and always pays his rent even when he is away. He keeps his room clean and tidy, but he does seem to have a number of lady friends. We sometimes discuss his latest girl when I make his dinner, and I tell him to be careful about the Italian girls.' Daphne doubted if Andrew needed much advice in that area, but was less interested in his social arrangements and more keen on establishing his present whereabouts.

'Does he work here in Rome?' she asked.

'Yes, I think so, at least during the time he is actually staying here. He goes off regularly in the mornings and comes back the same time each evening for a meal that I cook him.'

'Do you know where he works?'

'No, he never says much about his work, but he always wears a suit, so he must be respectable.'

'Can I see his room? I am a cousin and I haven't seen him for a long time. I should like to catch up with him.'

The concierge eyed Daphne up and down, 'All right,' she said, not really believing the relationship. 'I'll take you up.' The two of them climbed the wide ornate staircase to the first floor where the concierge unlocked the door. The flat inside comprised a sitting room and bedroom furnished quite comfortably and tastefully. In the bedroom there was a photograph of Veronica, the Maltese girl, sitting next to a handsome auburn-haired man with a beaming smile. So this must be Andrew! Daphne stared hard at the picture, making sure that she could recognise him when she caught up with him. The face that smiled back at her seemed innocent enough, and Daphne noticed with something of a twinge that she had the same snub nose, auburn hair and freckled face as her cousin, to whom she realised she must bear a considerable resemblance.

Daphne resumed her appraisal of the room to see if there was anything which might further her search for the room's wayward tenant. Suddenly, with a thrill, she saw that there was a telephone by the bed, and next to it pinned to the wall on a sheet of well-used paper was a list of telephone numbers. Most had girls' names against them, but one bore the magic word 'office'.

'I see that Andrew's office number is here,' she remarked to the concierge. 'Would you mind if I called his office from here to make an appointment to see him? I will of course pay for the call.' So saying she pressed a high denomination lire note into the lady's hand and swiftly got her approval.

She then sat down and dialled the number while the woman hovered interestedly across the room. The reply that she received came as quite a surprise to Daphne who was expecting some seedy commercial operation.

'International Relief Agency. How can I help you?' a polite Italian female voice said at the other end of the line. This was not the sort of office that Daphne had thought Andrew would be working in.

'I would like to speak to Mr Andrew Fletcher, please.'

'Do you know which department he is in?'

'I am afraid I don't.'

'Minuto, I will find out for you.'

After several minutes the voice came back. 'I am sorry, he is away on duty.'

'I am very keen to speak to him as I am a close relative and have come a long way to see him.'

'Minuto, I will see what I can do.'

An Italian 'minuto' was evidently longer than an English minute, but after a while a male voice with a strong accent took up the conversation.

'May I ask whom I am talking to?'

'Yes, I am Daphne Fleet, I am a cousin of Andrew Fletcher and I am anxious to see him as soon as possible.' There was a long pause at the other end.

'We don't have you down as a next of kin.'

'Well I'm not his next of kin, but I am related and I am very keen to see him.' There was another pause at the other end of the line.

'Perhaps you had better come and see me,' said the voice. 'If it is that urgent can you be here in, say, one hour from now?'

'Yes, certainly, that is very kind.'

'Good, my name is Peter van Hagen; ask for me at the reception desk.'

'Could you please tell me the address of the Agency?'

Mr van Hagen read out the address. 'I look forward to meeting you shortly. Goodbye, Miss Fleet.'

An hour later Daphne presented herself at the International Relief Agency, which was housed in a large, if somewhat neglected, building not too far away from Andrew's lodgings. She was ushered into a substantial office with a high ornate ceiling that had once been sumptuous but urgently needed a major facelift to bring it back to its former glory.

A large bald man rose from behind a desk to welcome her and offer her a seat.

'Pleased to meet you, Miss Fleet,' he said in what Daphne now recognised as a Dutch accent.

'It is kind of you to receive me at such short notice.'

'Why do you wish to see Mr Fletcher? You tell me he is your cousin, but that hardly seems a compelling reason to come so far so urgently.'

'His mother died recently, and I wished to offer my con-dolences and to discuss certain matters regarding his mother's will in which we were both beneficiaries.'

'Ah, I am Andrew's boss, and I do know that he requested

compassionate leave a few weeks ago to see his ailing mother. He was in Scotland for quite a while, looking after her on her death bed, and afterwards dealing with the funeral and the estate. He then went on holiday to Malta. However, I had a very urgent mission for him towards the end of this period, and I called him in Malta to see whether he would be prepared to cut his holiday short given that he had already been away for some time. He agreed to return to Rome and then flew straight off on the assignment, so I am afraid you cannot see him now, but I could arrange for a message to be forwarded to him. Is it a very private matter?'

Daphne thought quickly, 'Yes, it is. Would it be indiscreet to ask what mission Andrew is on?'

'Well I don't think that the mission itself is a secret, but first I should perhaps ask you if you appreciate what we do here?'

Daphne had to admit she did not.

'We are a non-profit organisation that acts as a co-ordinating body bringing together the diverse aid agencies that come from all over the world, offering a variety of help whenever there is a disaster, natural or otherwise, in almost any part of the globe. Sometimes we are passive, helping to make the most of whatever aid is on offer; sometimes we are more positive, trying to bring in a particular form of help that we know is needed in the disaster area, using our contacts and knowledge. The work usually involves at least one person going out to the area concerned.'

'That is a very laudable occupation,' Daphne told the Dutchman. 'Has my cousin been working with you for very long?'

'Oh, yes, many years. He is one of our more experienced workers, always keen to go on a mission, no matter how dangerous.'

Daphne was surprised to learn of Andrew's occupation and the high regard his superior had for him. Her opinion of

25

her cousin mellowed slightly, particularly now that it seemed that he had more than one motive for leaving Veronica.

'Where is that?'

'Well ... I suppose there is no reason why I shouldn't tell you. He is back in Croatia where he is supervising the return to normality in areas that were the scene of some of the worst fighting in the recent conflict ... I could arrange for a letter to be got to him.'

Daphne was somewhat nonplussed. She could not send a letter; she wanted to have the matter of the clock out with him face to face. There was nothing else for it, but she would have to go and find him.

'That is very kind of you, but I should like to see him in person.'

'I doubt if that would be possible. There is still a lot of animosity in the area between the different racial groups; a lot of people still have guns, there are landmines and the rule of law may not be readily enforceable in the outlying areas your cousin has to work in. Could you not wait until his tour of duty is finished?'

Daphne said that she could not, having only a limited amount of time available. The Dutchman could see that his visitor was very determined.

'Very well, I will show you on a map where he is working. We cannot give you any sort of authority for this visit and I must emphasise to you that this is a very unwise and danger-ous thing to do.'

The Dutchman then produced a map of Croatia and indi-cated where Andrew was based. His finger rested on a place with an unlikely combination of consonants. 'How do you pronounce that?' Daphne asked.

'I don't know any more than you do – I'm a Dutchman,' he smiled at her. 'He should be operating out of the local school. I will get a photostat of the map for you,' the official kindly offered, 'and let Andrew know you are coming.'

'I would appreciate the map and the address, but I would prefer if you did not let him know I am coming, just in case the journey proves too difficult and I have to turn back.'

'All right. How do you propose to get there? There are flights from Rome to Zagreb, the capital of Croatia, although they do make one stop on the way. There is a certain amount of public transport in Croatia, particularly trams, but where Andrew is things are more uncertain. We provided him with an agency vehicle at the airport and that forms part of the aid package.'

'I will go to Zagreb and see if I can hire or get a car.'

The Dutchman looked doubtful and shrugged his shoulders. 'Well, you are not my responsibility.' So saying, he gave her the copy of the map with the address, and wished her good luck and a safe journey.

Once outside Daphne knew exactly what she was going to do. On returning to her hotel she set about making some phone calls. Firstly she booked herself a flight to Zagreb – there was a seat on a plane leaving the next day. At the same time she also hired a car to be available at the airport at Zagreb – the best one they had. Daphne was a very self-confident driver and in a way looked forward to driving a good car in a different land. She had driven in Rome during her tour of duty there, and felt if she could do that, then she could drive anywhere.

Then she phoned her department at the Foreign Office in London. First she requested an extension of leave, which was provisionally granted without too much trouble. Next she asked to be put through to the Croatian section to obtain as much topical information as possible about the country. Basically they told her to stick to the main towns and tourist resorts and not to stray off into the interior, little more than she had expected. She also obtained the name of a contact at the British embassy in Zagreb, a Miss Johnson.

With what little time she had left in Rome Daphne used

her credit card to buy herself a smart black overcoat with a broad belt secured by a flamboyant brass buckle. She also bought a roll-necked sweater and a pair of leather trousers that she could not resist in one of the smartest of the many boutiques that seemed to abound, knowing that the benign autumn weather she was enjoying in Rome was unlikely to be paralleled in Croatia. She tried hard to think of what else she might need, but because she had little idea of what she might be facing in Croatia, she bought nothing but clothes.

4

The next morning saw her on the flight to Zagreb. For the first time she began to wonder more realistically what she would do and say if and when she finally caught up with Andrew. So far she had been motivated by a strong feeling of having been cheated and wanted as much as anything to give her guilty cousin a piece of her mind. She knew it was going to be difficult to get back the clock she felt was rightfully hers, although if she could only find a means of definitely proving her ownership, then she would have a better chance of retrieving it. But that would almost certainly mean that Andrew would have to admit his guilt. Daphne could see that there was not a lot of hope that he might do that. If he stuck to his guns and denied any knowledge of the switching of the two clocks there would be little she could do. He had the money, not the clock itself. Perhaps there might be a chink in his armour if she could discover what he had done with the proceeds, although even here he could say that the money formed part of his mother's inheritance.

As these thoughts sank in Daphne began to realise that what had started out as something of a crusade was in danger of becoming a hopeless cause. Her mood was not improved when the captain of the plane announced that he was beginning his descent into Zagreb where the temperature was just one degree above freezing.

On getting out of the plane Daphne pulled her new Italian overcoat around her. The air was clear and crisp, but very cold. The name of the country, Hrvatska in Croatian, was prominently displayed on the airport terminal, warning her that this was going to be a very different country from Italy, with a very different language. After passing through customs she found that the hired car she had ordered would not after all be available, so she found a taxi with a driver who had a smattering of English, and asked him to take her to a hotel in the centre of Zagreb. The drive proved quite lengthy as Zagreb turned out to be a sizeable city. The journey seemed far less hazardous than those in Rome and Malta partly because there was so much less traffic, but also because the main roads seemed so much wider. Only the many clanking trams which had traffic priority proved an obstacle. The hotel she was driven to seemed adequate for her needs as she hoped she would be spending only one night there. She booked a room without any difficulty, making sure that they would accept her credit card.

As soon as she had settled in, she phoned her contact at the British Embassy. It was Saturday, but Daphne managed to track her down. Miss Johnson accepted Daphne's invitation for a coffee and a chat in the hotel lounge as soon as she could come round.

Miss Johnson arrived half an hour later, a neatly dressed woman, probably in her fifties, with a down-to-earth attitude to life. They exchanged career histories briefly, Miss Johnson's being largely restricted to tours of duty in the capitals of former communist countries because of her ability to speak Russian which gave her an understanding of the other Slavonic languages of which Croatian was one. She was interested to learn of Daphne's proposed itinerary and advised her that the area where she was going was still unsettled, to say the least. For the third time Daphne was advised to keep to the main roads as far as possible as these were known to be safe, but to avoid straying into open country as there were still many land mines that had not yet been cleared. Miss Johnson did have one positive piece of information – she knew someone with a car to hire, and the car was a comfortable Mercedes. A quick telephone call arranged that this man would come to the hotel tomorrow morning.

'He is a Mr Punic, one of our contacts who we have used from time to time, and will probably give you a fair deal,' the embassy lady assured Daphne. 'And I will note where you are off to. If you want to phone in when you get there – if you can – I will try to help you if you have a problem. But I really must warn you again that you are heading into a troubled area where a woman by herself is bound to be a target of attention. I would warn you of men's attitude in the outlying districts to women on their own. They are regarded as fair game and rape has been a common offence throughout the troubled zones.' Miss Johnson was a career woman and a spinster who was giving her cautious advice with the best of intentions, but its impact on Daphne had the opposite effect. She looked at her colleague with her kind but rather plain face and her very severe clothes, and brushed aside the misgivings she had earlier felt on the plane, marshalling her inner will and resolved to go ahead, come what may. Now she was keen to get organised, so she thanked her colleague profusely and bade her goodbye; Miss Johnson left, shaking her head sadly as she feared the worst for her impetuous colleague.

Daphne had changed some money at the airport, but now found she could add to her supply of the local currency at the hotel where she was warned that the banks would be closed. She had brought with her some American dollars which she was holding as a reserve as she knew that western currencies were always acceptable in this part of Europe. By the time she finally set out to explore Zagreb it was already three in the afternoon. Most of the shops were closed for the weekend, but everywhere in the main squares the cafe bars were doing a roaring business. The inhabitants of Zagreb seemed to delight in spending a great deal of their time in animated conversation over a cup of thick, black strong coffee. With so little traffic apart from the trams, the main noise was the accumulated buzz of conversation from the cafes, which in some streets and squares occupied nearly every shop. Later, when it came to finding a restaurant for dinner, it was a different story. It seemed that the people of Zagreb went out to drink, but seldom to eat. Finally she found a restaurant with a menu in English and enjoyed a meal of locally caught fish followed by the inevitable black coffee.

The following morning, after a Croatian breakfast of cheese, cold meats, yogurt and coffee, Daphne was informed that she had a visitor. The man waiting for her in the lounge was middle-aged, quite tall and fair, and with at least two days' growth of beard on his chin.

'Are you Mr Punic, the gentleman with the Mercedes?' Daphne asked.

'Yes,' replied the bearded one, 'where is man to drive car?' His English was not good, but then Daphne spoke no Croatian.

'I am the person who wants to drive, and I have a current UK licence and a passport.'

The bearded Croatian was clearly put out. 'Man drive, not woman,' he told her. Daphne was beginning to see that Miss Johnson's warnings about men's attitudes in this part of the world had considerable substance. She decided to play her trump card. 'I will pay in US dollars. I think I will need the car for only three days, but I will pay for four.'

Mr Punic's attitude to women began to mellow. 'And you pay for insurance?'

Daphne agreed, and the Croatian named a price which was not too different from that of the airport rental company that had somehow failed to produce a vehicle. Fortunately

32

Daphne had enough dollars, which she handed over to the Croatian, receiving a firm handshake in return, plus a few forms in Croatian which she signed blindly.

'Now I show you how to drive Mercedes,' the Croatian said ingratiatingly, leading Daphne out into the street. Although at least ten years old, the Mercedes had been well looked after, and was one of the larger models. 'I show you controls.' He seated Daphne behind the wheel, and then lent all over her to point out each switch and button. 'Good,' he said 'Now we put petrol in – I drive.' They changed seats before driving the short distance to a filling station. Daphne paid for the petrol. On the way back to the hotel the Croatian allowed Daphne to take the wheel, telling her not to let the tank get too empty as it was not always easy to find a garage with the right sort of petrol. He also told her how much he valued his car and to be very careful where she parked it at night – if possible in a locked garage. As an afterthought he asked her where she was going, telling her that Eastern Croatia was not safe, at least not for his precious Mercedes. He then went on to give her very similar warnings about what might happen to his Mercedes as Daphne had already received concerning herself. One had to get one's priorities right here, Daphne thought, making a non-committal remark about her itinerary, reassuring him about the petrol and the parking before taking a note of his telephone number.

'You can phone me each evening to let me know car is OK or if you have problem,' he told her, making it abundantly clear where his concerns lay. Then he took his leave, turning back once to wave a little uncertainly as Daphne disappeared back into the hotel.

Now more than ever keen to get going, she packed her bag yet again, managing to get a large salami roll as emergency rations. She settled her bill with her card, at the same time securing a good road plan of Zagreb to add to the map of Croatia she had brought with her from Rome. Then she piled her luggage and herself into the quite luxurious Mercedes. A bright sunlight gave the stately old buildings in the many squares a romantic gloss as she drove out of the city centre. Although she had a reasonable amount of experience at driving on the right, it still took a time to get used to the traffic. Her biggest problem was to find her way out of the city when all the signs were in such an incredibly difficult language. Trust Andrew to choose a country like this! After half an hour of anxious driving with the help of the street plan provided by the hotel, she located the main road that was to take her from Zagreb into Eastern Croatia.

All she had to do now was to keep on this road, which, according to the map the Dutchman had given her, would take her within a few miles of her destination. She settled down to a steady drive, cursing each time she got caught behind a battered old Yugo saloon puffing out fumes as it struggled to make thirty miles an hour, or alternatively a horse-drawn cart piled high with agricultural produce.

The map showed she had about 150 kilometres to cover before she had to turn off the main road, with only a few miles of minor roads before she reached her destination, Bjelovska. She was sure she could make it before darkness fell. Although the address she had been given in Bjelovska was the local school, which she felt should not be hard to locate, she was anxious not to have to search for it in the dark.

After an hour and a half of fairly relaxed driving through a flat agricultural landscape she came across a restaurant. Remembering how difficult it had been to find one in Zagreb she decided to have a break, not least because she needed a visit to the toilet. The menu was almost meaningless, no one spoke English, but she managed to order soup, bread and yogurt, buying a bottle of water for later.

Resuming her journey, she noticed that the bright sunshine had disappeared to be replaced by some menacing dark clouds. A few more miles and the rain started, which soon turned to sleet and then increasingly to snow. Visibility was badly reduced, forcing Daphne to drive with the lights on. She was well pleased with the Mercedes which had a good heating system and was coping well with the deteriorating conditions outside. The fact that she could scarcely see the road signs was not so much of a problem as most of them were a meaningless jumble of consonants to her anyway. Occasionally a village would have a really short name like Boz, which she could identify on the map open on the seat beside her.

Visibility worsened. The snow was beginning to settle on the road. Traffic became sparser but the going was slower. Daphne's spirits drooped. Stupidly she had not reckoned with bad weather; the warnings she had received had concentrated on her personal safety, or in the case of the owner of the Mercedes, the safety of the car. She stopped in order to work out how much further she had to drive – only another fifty miles. She decided to battle on.

Forty miles to go and the Mercedes was responding well to the thickening snow on the road, its tyres biting easily.

Thirty miles and she was still able to follow the tracks of preceding vehicles. Twenty miles and she came up behind a slow-moving lorry. They came to a hill with both vehicles creeping up it in bottom gear. Daphne's heart was in her mouth lest the lorry got stuck, but agonisingly slowly both finally made the summit.

Ten miles and she knew she must start watching out for the junction where she had to turn off the main road. Fortunately, the windscreen wipers were doing a good job with the snow. At last she spotted the place name she was looking for, partly obscured by snow, but definitely the junction where she must leave the main road. Although snowing heavily and with limited visibility it was fortunately still daylight.

Because of the snow it was difficult for Daphne to judge the condition of the side road, but at least it was level and appeared quite straight, unlike most English country roads. The Mercedes' tyres were still gripping the road and she felt reasonably optimistic. After a short distance, an isolated building with what looked like the word *Kavana* loomed up out of the snow. 'Cafe,' thought Daphne, 'that's one Croatian word I have learnt'. On the spur of the moment she decided to pull up in order to see if she could get any directions to Bjelovska, and the school. She decided not to pull too far into the side of the road in case there were any unseen obstructions under the snow, and to leave the engine running. She realised she had little chance of being understood, but she took her map and a couple of American dollars with her in the hope that they might improve international relations.

Pulling on her Italian overcoat, she ran across to the door, pushed it open and walked in. The room, although quite large, was scantily furnished with a few meagre tables and chairs. One or two empty bottles and glasses stood on the tables, there were a few torn pictures on the walls advertising drinks, and the whole place had a depressingly derelict feeling. Behind a very small bar on one side an equally small bald-headed man with the regulatory two days' growth of beard stood reading a newspaper. In one corner was a lighted stove round which sat two shabbily-dressed younger men, also with the usual two days' growth of beard. They were talking together in guttural voices.

Daphne asked the man behind the counter if he spoke any English. She got no reply. She produced a dollar and the map. The man was implacable. He just looked blankly ahead saying nothing. But one of the two men in the corner got up, opened the door, looked out, came back and began talking agitatedly to his companion.

Then the situation changed abruptly. The same man got

up again quickly, grabbed Daphne's arm and shoulder and began to force her towards the front door. The man behind the counter disappeared into a back room. Daphne struggled desperately. The second man had also risen and was moving towards her and the door. Daphne saw a bottle on a table as she was being dragged towards the door. Frantically she grabbed it with her free hand, smashed the neck, and plunged the jagged glass into the man's face. Blood spurted out, the man released his grip on Daphne and put his hands to his face, screaming.

The second man was now standing by the front door, blocking the way out. Daphne turned and ran to the back of the room where there was another door. It opened readily and Daphne burst out into an open back yard surrounded by a high fence. Everything was covered by the snow which was still falling heavily. Another door was at the end of the yard. She rushed across to it and again she was lucky, as it opened easily. She glanced back briefly – neither man had yet appeared – before plunging through the door and out into open country. She ran as hard as she could in the thick snow, glancing over her shoulder every now and again to see if she was being followed. There was no sign of anyone coming. Although the snow made it easy to get out of view her tracks would be bound to give her away. After a few minutes she stopped behind a low bush to recover her breath. There was still no sign of her pursuers.

Then she heard an unmistakable sound – an engine being revved up – followed by the equally unmistakable roar of a car being driven away rapidly. She had left the engine of the Mercedes running with the keys in the dashboard because she thought she would not be stopping more than a minute or two. The two men must have decided to play their luck and go for the car rather than for her.

In the time it took to recover her breath she began to think more rationally again. Fortunately she had put on her Italian overcoat before she went into the *Kavana*, and for the time being at least the violent exercise she had been obliged to take had got the blood coursing through her veins, but she knew she could not stay out too long in this weather with the light fading as night approached. Visibility was in any case very limited.

As she began to work out what her next course of action should be and her brain started to register again, something was stirring in the back of her mind. What was it that the lady at the embassy had warned her against? Mines! Don't stray off the roads she had told her, there are still uncleared mines in some areas in the east.

Daphne looked about her. She had already run unthinkingly across at least one hundred yards of open country blanketed with snow where it was impossible to tell what was underneath. Now she was sheltering in a clump of bushes. Should she retrace her steps back to the *Kavana* in the hope that having missed the mines once, she would also miss them again going back? She could not be certain of placing her feet in exactly the same footsteps on the way back and the snow was starting to blur her footprints anyway. She decided to try to work her way through the bushes back to the road in the hope that mines would not have been laid in such a difficult terrain. Choosing the biggest bushes which she could actually force her way through, she began the nerve-racking walk back to the road. With her heart in her mouth and her overcoat wrapped round her to protect her from the undergrowth she gingerly made her way forward until she finally reached the edge of the road, where she could see the *Kavana* again in the distance. The Mercedes was indeed gone. What to do now? Everything she possessed was in the car.

The man in the *Kavana* might be in league with the other two so she might place herself at risk if she went back. She decided to walk down the road towards where she thought the village might be, thinking bitterly that the warnings she had received had come true, but realising with mixed feelings that in choosing to take either the car or her, the two men had chosen the car. She was under no illusion that if they had really wanted to, they could have caught up with her without much difficulty. But at least one of them would carry the scars of his assault for a considerable time to come, and the thought gave Daphne some bitter satisfaction.

It was still snowing heavily, and now that the initial rush of excitement was over, she began to feel extraordinarily weary. Her arm and shoulder where she had been grabbed and pulled along were aching and throbbing. She could make out little of her surroundings except that they appeared to be mostly flat fields with only a few patches of uncultivated land. Perhaps there were some farms here? After all, Andrew was supposed to be helping with the rehabilitation of a village.

She had not walked more than a few hundred yards when she heard a blood-chilling sound somewhere ahead of her – a high-pitched howling, made more intense and compelling by the otherwise complete silence brought about by the blanket of snow that was enveloping everything. She tried to peer through the wall of snow.

'My God, are there wolves in these parts? I thought they had died out with Dracula,' she thought to herself. Already cold, the eerie sound made her shiver as she listened intently, hoping against hope that the agonised wailing would not be repeated.

But it was. This time in a totally different tone, more like a low growl, almost as if it came from a different species of animal. And the sound was definitely nearer – whatever it was that was making these awful chilling animal howls was coming her way, although exactly from which direction she could not tell as the snow had a curious distorting effect. She looked about her to see if perhaps there was a tree she could climb into, or anything that would enable her to get some protection from whatever mysterious animal was roaming the snowy waste around her, but there was nothing but flat agricultural land. Again the nerve-racking noise came, quite close now, repeated several times like the bark of a dog. Daphne stood quite still, shivering from both fear and cold, not knowing what to do. She cast around to see if there might be a stick or stone she could use as a defensive weapon, but the snow covered everything and she could see nothing that might be of help. The mesmeric howling came again, this time several quite different sounds, and very much closer.

And then out of the murk in front of her, moving silently in the snow, there appeared a pack of dogs. It was difficult to say who was more surprised by the encounter. The dogs came to an abrupt halt on the edge of visibility in the snow, not more than fifteen yards away. They were a motley lot, perhaps seven or eight in all, one undoubtedly an alsatian and quite big, but several others quite small, and each one a different breed or mixture of breeds. They were such a curious collection, clearly not the wolves that Daphne had originally feared, that her horror and loathing left her. While the animals stood there in silence, Daphne made the first move. Shouting at the top of her voice and waving her arms she moved towards her canine tormentors. They were no heroes. They quite literally turned tail and disappeared silently into the snow in the direction from which they had come. Daphne breathed a sigh of relief, pushing her hands, which were still shaking, deep into the pockets of her overcoat.

She set out again, the snow covering her shoes and blowing into her eyes. But a wave of nausea suddenly overcame her and she began shivering uncontrollably. The effort and excitement of the last hour combined with the mauling she had received in the *Kavana* proved too much for her. She collapsed on the road and passed into unconsciousness. The snow was still falling...

5

Daphne could feel herself regaining consciousness and opened her eyes to find herself in a strange room. She was lying on a simple metal bed with a mattress and two old blankets over her. She was still wearing the same clothes she had on when she collapsed except that her shoes had been removed. Her shoulder still ached and her mouth felt horribly dry. The room appeared to be a classroom, although it had only chairs and no desks, but there was a blackboard with words chalked up in the usual indecipherable Croatian language. It was now daylight so she assumed she had passed the night here. She looked at her watch – ten past eight – she supposed that must be morning. She propped herself up on her elbows and looked around further. There was a glass partition between her room and the next and someone was walking about outside. Daphne called out.

The door opened and in walked a tall auburn-haired freckle-faced man in his forties. He was broad-shouldered and dressed in a rough sweater and jeans. Daphne recognised him instantly – he was the man in the photo in the Rome flat, the man she had been so desperately searching for these last two weeks.

'Andrew Fletcher!' she called out excitedly.

The man was astounded. 'How on earth do you know my name?' he asked in amazement.

'You are Andrew Fletcher, then?'

'Yes I am, but who are you?'

'I'm your long-lost cousin Daphne Fleet, and I've been searching for you in I don't know how many different places. You're not an easy man to track down, but I'm glad I have found you at last.'

'Well, Daphne, I'm very pleased to meet you – but I would point out that it was I who found you. Had I not been driving back at the crucial time on that road, I doubt if you would have survived very long out there. Anyway I'm glad to see that you've come round. I thought it best to let you sleep once I was sure that you were alive. How do you feel now?'

'Well, I have a sore shoulder, but I think I'm otherwise OK.'

'Good. I daresay you could do with a cup of coffee. I'll see what I can rustle up in the kitchen. There are primitive toilet facilities up the stairs over there – only cold water, I'm afraid. When you've finished come and join me in the kitchen at the other end and tell me how you came to be lying on an obscure Croatian road.'

Daphne cleaned herself up as best she could before joining Andrew in the kitchen. As she had lost her make-up kit with everything else in the car, she could not even brush her hair. Her clothes were crumpled from having slept in them. She looked at herself in the broken mirror with dismay – what would Andrew think of her like this?

'Where are we?' she asked when she returned downstairs.

'Well, we're in the village of Bjelovska, and this is the village school. It was supposed to be my job to help get things going again here, but I fear I've come too soon. There's no teacher and few if any children. Virtually everything has been looted. I work for the International Relief Agency, and I'm supposed to be co-ordinating things, but there is no relief and very few people at the moment to be helped. Also there don't seem to be any local people in charge. The situation is

42

very fluid – one day it seems things are getting better, but then the position deteriorates. I'm none too happy about the lack of any law or order here. My job isn't to restore order, but to help out once the situation has settled. I propose to pack up and come back again when the villagers return, and there's someone to keep things going afterwards here. Here's a cup of hot coffee, and some sort of salami and mangolds that I've heated up – it's the best I can do in the circumstances.' After a pause, Andrew continued 'I don't know whether you know that my mother died a few weeks ago. I didn't invite you or your mother to the funeral as I had lost contact with you, but I believe the executors were trying to find you. Also I know that your mother and mine hadn't seen each other for many years. Now tell me how you came to be here. Has your visit anything to do with my mother's death?'

The moment of truth had come for Daphne. She had spent so much time and effort to find her cousin, but now that she had unexpectedly caught up with him she was unsure of herself. How could she question him about the clock, when he had just saved her life? But then again he did not know who she was when he rescued her, and rescuing people was his job. She looked at him hard. He did not look a rogue, in fact he looked quite handsome despite the fact that like every other man in this part of the world he had a growth of beard. Daphne drank her coffee and began her story.

'Well,' she said, 'my presence here is in fact to do with your mother's death. In her will she left me the old clock in her lounge on which she taught me to tell the time. I happen to know that this clock is quite valuable. I also remember the clock very well even after all these years. When I came to collect it from the solicitors who were the executors, the clock they gave me was definitely not the one your mother owned, it was an inferior one.'

'Well, that's very strange,' Andrew replied, 'because I too remember the clock well. It was a London maker musical

43

bracket clock. All the other furniture was left to me as the only child, but I know that it was willed to you so I left it to the solicitors for them to pass on to you.'

Daphne was taken aback by this unexpected statement, and didn't know what to say.

'I hope that you didn't think that I had swapped the clocks and then flogged the good one and scarpered with the proceeds.'

'Well,' admitted Daphne, 'that's exactly what I did think and that's why I am here.'

'Oh dear. Well, I can assure you that I arranged for the clock to be collected by the solicitors, although it never occurred to me to ask for a receipt at the time . . . I just had all the other furniture delivered to an auction, asking them to leave the clock. Later the cottage itself was to be sold. I can't understand what could have happened.'

Daphne was in a quandary. Andrew showed no sign of guilt as he told her his story and she felt increasingly inclined to believe him. She decided not to mention that she had seen the very clock for sale in a local antique shop. But if he had not swapped the clocks what had happened? Daphne was beginning to feel she had come all this way and was no further forward with her inheritance.

'I don't really know what to think, Andrew,' Daphne admitted. 'Clearly I will have to go back to Scotland to find out what has happened.'

'Well, if it will help you think any better of me I will come with you, with your permission of course. I'm not doing any good here and I ought to find out how the sale of the cottage is proceeding. It's difficult for them to keep in touch with me as I move about so much. As far as my job is concerned there is often a gap between one tour of duty and another when I usually catch up on my office work. I'm sure that can wait. I've been working for the Agency for long enough now for them to give me a certain amount of latitude – it is not as if I get paid a whacking great salary. Only if there were a major tragedy would I not be allowed to leave.'

'Are you alone here, then?'

'Yes, I am. Various donor organisations come and go, but I am the only non-local here at present. Oh, by the way, how's your Croatian?'

'Non-existent.'

'And you still haven't told me how you came to be lying unconscious down the road here.'

Daphne related her story as briefly as she could, telling him only about the journey from Rome onwards.

'And so you see I am destitute in a foreign country,' she finished.

'Well, I have some more bad news for you. Yours wasn't the only car stolen. The Agency vehicle disappeared in the night. It looks as if we are marooned here for the time being. At least it has stopped snowing, and I have a few basic supplies here. But I'm none too happy about our being stuck out here alone, particularly now the Agency vehicle has gone. I don't know how to get out of here. We are unlikely to find a telephone that works and neither of us speaks Croatian.'

They both sat a while saying nothing and sipping coffee. Across the room was a large ornate mirror, miraculously still intact. They happened to look into it together and then smiled at each other. Each knew what the other was thinking.

'There isn't much doubt that we are related, is there?' said Andrew, reading Daphne's thoughts. Daphne for her part was beginning to warm to her cousin, and began to feel guilt about all the unpleasant ideas that she had of him, although she still had no proof that his story about the clock was true. But his offer to go back to Scotland with her made her inclined to give him the benefit of the doubt and she welcomed the idea of a companion when she got back to Scotland.

They began to discuss what they should do, without coming up with any very concrete solutions. The best they could think of was to walk the several miles to the main road and either hitch a lift or find a working telephone. At least Andrew had a minimum of provisions, his bag with some clothes and a little Croatian money.

'All I have are the clothes I stand up in – oh, and two American dollars. Everything I had was in the car,' Daphne gloomily informed him.

They talked about their childhood in Scotland together.

'Do you know I always looked up to you?' said Daphne.

'Well, I must be two years older than you and I am still a few inches taller.' The conversation carried on for a while as they exchanged reminiscences of their early days and told each other of their respective careers. Daphne had certainly seen something of the world in the Foreign Office, but Andrew's life, they agreed, had been the more adventurous. He listed the various places he had been sent to around the world, which made Daphne rather envious. Then he told her about the usually atrocious conditions he had to work in, and the dreadful plight of the people he was sent to help. Surely this could not be the man who would steal my clock, thought Daphne. And yet…

'What about Veronica?' Daphne asked. 'Is that the way you treat all your lady friends?' She didn't like to tell him that she had been in his flat and seen just how many girls he knew.

'You know about her then?'

Daphne told him of her trip to Malta.

'I met her last year on holiday, and we got on well together, but until my mother died, I had very little money to think about setting up a home. Now my finances are improving, I thought I might make a go of it with Veronica, although that would probably mean giving up my job. Then I got the call from my boss to come here, and I couldn't resist the temptation to move on again. I hope she didn't take it too badly?'

Daphne told him frankly of her chat with Veronica.

46

They spent so much time reminiscing together that it was now approaching midday.

'We ought to do something more positive,' Daphne told him. But just then they heard a noise that was to make up their minds for them. It was the sound of an approaching car.

'Good,' said Andrew, 'now perhaps we can get out of here.' He began to cross the room to the door while Daphne got up to peer out of the snow-encrusted window. What she saw made her draw back in alarm. The car pulling up in front of the school was a large black Mercedes, and although she could not see the number plate as it was sideways on she was sure this was the same car that she had hired. She watched discreetly from behind the frosty window as three men got out of the vehicle. As they turned to walk towards the school Daphne saw that one of them had livid fresh scars on his face. Undoubtedly he was the man who had attacked her yesterday, and she was fairly sure that one of the other two men was the second man from the cafe, although she did not recognise the third man.

'Get down,' she commanded in an urgent whisper to Andrew. 'It's the men from the cafe who attacked me yesterday.' Andrew ducked down as he was told. 'We must hide somehow,' she said. 'These men mean business and they certainly aren't going to be pleased to see me.'

'Well, there's little enough place to hide,' Andrew replied. 'It's only a small school. There's the larger room downstairs that was presumably some sort of assembly hall. There's definitely no cover there. There's the room you slept in, another similar room and the kitchen. We'd better go upstairs and hope that they will go away. The place has already been ransacked.'

As they spoke, the three men outside approached a small outhouse where the door was still shut. The man with the scars drew out from his coat a wicked-looking knife and proceeded to kick in the door. All three then went inside the outhouse.

Andrew and Daphne took the opportunity of their momentary disappearance to hurry upstairs.

'There are four rooms up here,' he told Daphne, 'none of them very big, but each has a cupboard. Oh, and there's the bathroom.' All the doors to the rooms were wooden in the lower half and glass in the upper half, so that it was easy to see into each room.

'Looks as if our only hope is to hide either in one of the cupboards,' or in the bathroom. There are no locks anyway, except in the bathroom, and that doesn't work.'

'They might want to use the loo, so let's try one of the cupboards, Daphne said. 'But I can't see what we can do if they find us. We're outnumbered and at least one of them has a knife. And I can't believe that they will be merciful to us.'

They heard the three men come in through the front door and the sound of furniture being thrown about. From their footsteps they judged that they had moved into the kitchen. 'That's a give-away – they'll realise from the food and drink on the table that someone has been here recently,' Andrew moaned.

The men seemed to spend some time in the kitchen, but after a while Daphne and Andrew heard them going back out into the open. Andrew crept out of the cupboard and peered through a corner of the window. The three men were carrying various provisions they had found in the kitchen out to the car. Not much of a haul there, he thought.

Unfortunately, as soon as they had deposited their loot the men returned. For some time they carried on a conversation in the kitchen, but then the unmistakeable footsteps of at least two of them clumping up the stairs caused Andrew and Daphne to cringe back in the cupboard.

'If only two come upstairs we might just have a chance to take them by surprise,' whispered Andrew rather forlornly.

The two men smashed their way through the rooms upstairs, deliberately breaking the glass in the doors. After what seemed an age they came into the room where Andrew and Daphne were hiding. 'This is it,' thought Daphne, 'now or never.'

At that very moment, there was the sound of another car approaching. The man downstairs called out to the two upstairs. Daphne and Andrew listened with bated breath as the men's footsteps receded and then clattered downstairs. The two listened intently as the car stopped and the engine was turned off. 'I wonder if they are friend or foe,' whispered Daphne. 'Let's just see what they look like. If they look at all respectable we might be able to attract their attention.'

The two crept to the window and watched as three men climbed out of the second car, now parked behind the first. Curiously, this car was also a black Mercedes and looked very like the first.

The three men from inside the school came out to face the new arrivals. Not only was scarface brandishing a knife, but each of his companions also had one. The three newcomers came to a halt in front of the two cars, and it soon became clear that relations between the two groups were certainly not going to be friendly, with both of them gesticulating and shouting at the tops of their voices. The argument between the two groups went on for some time with the confrontation becoming increasingly aggressive.

'I don't fancy the chances of the new lot,' whispered Andrew. 'For a start they look too well-dressed and they don't appear to be armed. I think I will go down to give them a hand. It might help to even things up a bit and I might be able to create a diversion.'

Before Daphne could say or do anything Andrew started off downstairs. She watched out of the window as the three men with knives prepared to launch an attack on the other three. The newcomers had bunched together defensively, and just as their opponents moved in with their knives one of them drew a very large automatic gun from his coat and fired several shots at the feet of their attackers who halted abruptly. Waving his gun at the three knifemen the newcomer was making it very plain that they had better back off. He fired another round of shots and the three broke off the engagement, finally running off down the road and disappearing, leaving both cars behind.

At this point Andrew appeared at the doorway. Daphne rushed down to join him as he started a conversation in English with one of the men, whom Daphne immediately recognised. It was Mr Punic, the owner of the Mercedes.

'Am I glad to see you!' beamed Daphne, introducing him to Andrew.

'And I am very glad to see my Mercedes,' replied the doughty Croatian, laughing. 'These are my two brothers, and that is one of our other Mercedes. It looks as if we arrive just in time.'

'Well, you couldn't have left it much longer as far as we were concerned. But how did you find us?'

'That's easy. As you must understand, not very many women drive here in Croatia yet and I am not used to hiring out my Mercedes to a lady. In your country women drive all time, but not so much here. I was unhappy about hiring car to you, and when you did not phone in last night I became more worried. I know that when people hire car there is no need to phone in, but I just felt I had to know what was going on. So first thing this morning I phoned Miss Johnson at the Embassy to see if she could tell me where you might be. When she told me where you were going I was horrified. I knew there is trouble in this area and that bands of all types of bad people were stealing and raping. So I phoned my two brothers – they are in the same business I am – and we set off down here as fast as we could. It is a good car the Mercedes, and we weren't worried about speed limits. We timed our arrival exactly right.'

Daphne and Andrew agreed with him. 'Let's see what damage they have done to my Mercedes.' The five of them walked over to the car and inspected it. Apart from being covered in snow and slush it seemed OK. Andrew peered into the back seat and saw some of his kit that had been looted by the knifemen and thrown there.

'If you don't mind,' he said, 'I'd like to try to find the rest of my stuff, and then I think we ought to leave this area as soon as possible.'

Mr Punic was in a good mood. 'That's fine,' he said, climbing into the driving seat of his car to start the engine. 'Sounds good,' he said and his smile widened. He opened the bonnet to listen knowingly to the engine running. Then he opened the boot. To everyone's surprise Daphne's bag and other items were still there.

'These men were not Croatians,' explained Mr Punic. 'They had a lucky break in finding my car. They were going to use it to fill it up with whatever else they could loot and then clear off.'

Once Mr Punic had got his most pressing matter resolved he enquired how Daphne had been robbed and how she was. He also discussed the general situation with Andrew. It was decided it was too risky to try to find the stolen Agency vehicle, which might have been taken by a totally different group. When Andrew had got all his things together Daphne asked if they would mind waiting while she changed and tidied herself up after her gruelling experience. Never one to spend much time on make-up, she was ready in ten minutes. Andrew cast an admiring eye over his cousin before making ready to go back to Zagreb.

'One thing more,' said Mr Punic as Daphne and Andrew went to get into the car. 'I drive.'

Almost immediately after the two cars started out they passed the cafe where Daphne's horrific experiences had begun the previous afternoon. She pointed it out to Mr

51

Punic. 'It's not worth stopping,' he said. 'Even if the owner is not in league with the other three bandits, I doubt if he will know anything and will be too frightened to say much if he does.' Strangely, the place now had quite a picturesque appearance, with everything covered in snow and sparkling in the midday sun, so different from yesterday.

'And we won't bother with the police,' added Mr Punic. 'They might want to know where our gun came from.'

Mr Punic was in a cheerful mood, pointing out the various places of interest, but then bemoaning the damage caused to some of the houses in the recent troubles. When they came to a restaurant just off the main road he pulled up and the five of them trooped in. 'I am going to treat you to a true Croatian meal,' he told Daphne and Andrew, 'and to start with we will have some local wine.' When they were all seated at a table Mr Punic ordered the food and drink for all of them. As the menu was totally unintelligible to the English couple they tried guessing the contents of each course, but with only limited success.

Fortified by a good meal and a liberal quantity of wine Mr Punic was even more cheerful as they resumed their journey back to Zagreb. But Andrew was more thoughtful. 'I'm thinking what I'm going to report back to my office in Rome,' he explained to Daphne. 'I've lost our vehicle, although in all fairness we would have left it there as part of the aid package. And I have to make up my mind whether to advise delaying sending any more help in – I never like doing that.'

Daphne for her part felt curiously divided in spirit; deflated on the one hand to think she had come so far for so little, yet somehow increasingly elated by the attachment she was feeling towards her cousin sitting next to her, whom she had so reviled before she met him.

'That was very brave of you, to go down unarmed to join in the fight,' she admiringly told him.

'Well, after your successful battle with old scarface I felt I had to keep the side up,' he replied modestly.

They reached Zagreb without further incident, Mr Punic driving them back to the same hotel that Daphne had started out from. As they were saying their goodbyes he had one further surprise for them.

'This week it will be December 6th. This is a special time of the year for us in Croatia. It would be an honour if you would join me and my family in a celebration at my home.'

That's very kind. I am sure we should both like that.'

'Good. I'll pick you up at seven. You can wear whatever you like.' Then he drove off with his two brothers.

After Daphne and Andrew had booked into the hotel again they decided that they had better rest for an hour or two in order to sleep off the heavy late lunch and to prepare themselves for the evening. Mr Punic duly arrived in his familiar Mercedes at the arranged time to be welcomed by Daphne dressed in the only skirt she had brought, together with a reasonably low-cut sweater, while Andrew had a very English-looking blazer. They drove to his home, which was a quite substantial flat in an uninspiring modern block in a suburb of Zagreb. Mr Punic had a large family, all of whom seemed delighted to welcome his new friends and to practise their English. The conversation was helped by liberal supplies of local beer and spirits – Mr Punic's family was clearly not on the wagon or anywhere remotely near it. The celebrations became somewhat blurred in Daphne's mind as the evening proceeded, but when the time came for Andrew and her to be taken home, she had acquired quite a few new Croatian friends, even if her knowledge of Croatian customs had scarcely advanced.

Daphne found it difficult to get to sleep that night – maybe it was all that rather exotic drink she had somehow failed to resist, but more probably it was the aftermath of the excitement of the last few days. She decided to review her

53

position so far in order to help her to get to sleep.

Firstly and positively she had found the man she had been looking for. And, as she had always feared he would, he denied switching the clocks. He had a very honest appearance with a job that seemed to imply a degree of integrity. She felt inclined to believe him, and after all he had saved her life! Yet there was something more to her feelings about his character, almost as if the two of them knew what the other was thinking – a mutual telepathy. But this telepathy did not go as far as Daphne knowing what Andrew thought of her. He had been very convivial and attentive at the party, but then he had had quite a lot to drink. He was certainly a 'likeable chap' and she could understand that his handsome appearance, his rather swashbuckling yet sympathetic job and his general easygoing nature could result in the lengthy list of girls' telephone numbers she had found in his flat in Rome. Should she let her number be added to the list? And he had somehow talked his way into going back to Scotland with her. Was this a genuine desire to help, or was he going in order to try to cover up his tracks? The more she thought about it the less certain she became: her heart said one thing but her head said she should be more cautious. Anyway, she was committed now.

So what should be done on arrival in Scotland? At what stage of events could the clock have been switched? Should she try to trace the movement of the clock back to her aunt's cottage? Go back to the woman in the antique shop to find out if she could offer any help as to who exactly sold it to her? There were two sets of auctioneers or agents involved, one selling the contents other than the clock, and one selling the cottage itself. Both must have had access to the property and both probably employed staff. She had better check with both of these. The trouble with each of these lines of enquiry was the same as the enquiries with Andrew – a simple denial or a 'don't know anything about it' reply could not really be disproved. Nevertheless she decided to have a go at the two agents to start with, and with this settled in her mind, she fell into a deep sleep.

The next morning she met Andrew for the Croatian breakfast that she was starting to acquire a taste for. He had to go back to Rome and thought he might be a couple of days there before he could fly back to the UK. Daphne decided to spend one more day in Zagreb before flying back to London, hoping her shoulder which was still sore would heal itself without the need for medical assistance. They therefore agreed to meet at Daphne's home in London in two days' time when Andrew's work in Rome was finished, and set about booking the necessary flights. Fortunately it was a time of the year when there was very little tourist traffic, so they were able to book seats on the appropriate planes without any problem other than the cost. Daphne rang her mother to tell her all was well, that she would be coming back soon, and that she had at last found Andrew whom she had invited back to Fulham to spend a night with them before going on to Scotland. She decided to omit some of the more hair-raising parts of her travels in order not to upset her mother.

Andrew flew back to Rome that afternoon, leaving Daphne to explore Zagreb. Despite the problems of an incomprehensible language it was an easy city to get around in. The centre was partially pedestrianised, giving it a sense of tranquility so lacking in London or Rome. Finding a restaurant for a meal proved something of a problem as most of the local inhabitants seemed to confine themselves to sipping thick black coffee in the cafes, hardly any of which provided anything to eat.

The following day was spent strolling round the tree-lined squares and backstreet shops. She bought two pairs of Italian shoes – shoe shops were everywhere in a country where people had yet to be overwhelmed by the motor car. Because she had no one to talk to she found her mind repeatedly being filled with thoughts of Andrew, so that by the end of the day she was quite looking forward to renewing their acquaintance in Fulham.

6

Back in London, Daphne was once again seated in her comfortable lounge at home, telling her mother of her experiences of the last few days.

'I'm glad that it seems as if Andrew is not to blame,' said her mother, 'I must say I was very apprehensive when you first told me about the clock, and you would have been in an awkward position if it had turned out that he had taken it and refused to hand it back or give you the money. And I shall look forward to meeting him after all these years, when he comes here. I wonder if I will recognise him.'

'I think you will,' thought Daphne, knowing how alike the two of them were.

For the second time in the last couple of weeks Daphne prepared herself for the drive to Scotland. One of the first things she undertook was to take the MG round to her local garage to have the optional luggage rack fitted to the back of the car. Space was going to be at a premium with the two of them in the car. She also had Andrew added to her insurance – she decided to let him take a turn at the wheel. The last drive had been quite taxing for her in the poor weather. She kitted herself out as she had for the first trip, concentrating on clothes that would be warm without being bulky. She could not resist taking her new Italian overcoat which she had found so effective in Croatia, but decided to restrict herself to only one heavy-duty sweater. She found herself hoping that these thick warm clothes would not make her look too unattractive to her cousin; but then her appearance in Croatia had not exactly been flattering, yet he seemed not to be repelled.

Andrew arrived at 93 Woodlands Park Road later that evening. He carried the minimum of luggage – he had learned from his many journeys around the world how to cram all he needed into one quite small bag. Daphne welcomed him warmly with a kiss and introduced him to her mother.

'You were just a very young schoolboy when I last saw you all those years ago,' she told him, 'but I can see the likeness to your mother and to Daphne here. I'm sorry now that your mother and I lost contact with each other. Anyway, you're very welcome here tonight. I've cooked a shoulder of English lamb which might make a change from all this exotic foreign food that I'm sure you have on your travels. Daphne has told me what you do, but I shall be very interested to hear about your exploits over dinner.'

A few minutes later they were seated round the table while Andrew recounted some of his more adventurous assignments, as well as the rather sad circumstances of his mother's death and funeral. It transpired that Andrew himself rarely had the opportunity to visit his mother in Scotland, but invariably found time to write to her from the various countries he visited. Andrew's father had died shortly after he was born, so his mother had remained a solitary widow just like Daphne's mother, and was therefore always pleased to hear from her son. During the conversation Daphne gave Andrew the vital piece of information about seeing the clock in the window of the antique shop. They intended to have an early night ready for the morning, but it was past midnight before they all got to bed.

The following morning they decided against an early start in order to avoid the rush-hour congestion, allowing themselves instead the pleasure of a leisurely English breakfast prepared by Daphne's mother. At ten o'clock they piled their luggage into and onto the little red MG and then set off to the M1, tediously threading their way through suburban traffic, with Daphne at the wheel. On their way out she saw the old number 29 bus that she knew so well, catching a fleeting glimpse of the rather bleak faces of all those passengers on their daily routines.

'This is a bit more exciting than the good old number 29,' Daphne told Andrew as they made their way northwards, and he settled his long frame into the leather upholstery.

'While you're concentrating on the driving I'll run through our options,' he said. 'Firstly and obviously there's what I'll call plan A – that is to pay a visit to the lady in the antique shop. If we can find out from her from whom she bought the clock, then we are more or less home and dry as regards the guilty party. It may even be that she switched the clock. I suppose she could have obtained access to the cottage and then exchanged the clocks there. She could have bought the other clock in the antique trade. But would she blatantly display it in her window if she got it illegally? There is the point that it may have passed through more than one pair of hands, but we should be well on the way to tracing who originally did the dirty work.' It was clear Andrew had been thinking along similar lines to Daphne. 'There is one major flaw with plan A. The person who would be the loser in all this would be the lady in the shop. Even if she came by the clock legitimately, she would have to give it up, and try to get her money back from whoever sold it to her. And if that person is a criminal, as he presumably is, then her chances might not be all that good. So in order to reinforce our case we might find ourselves having to go to the police in the hope that they might put pressure on her to reveal her seller. In any case we are going to have to get some sort of documentation to prove our ownership.'

'I think you mean my ownership,' Daphne corrected him.

'Yes. And a copy of the will or a solicitor's letter which just mentions a clock isn't going to be all that convincing.'

'And the lady is going to be even more unwilling to give up the clock than you think, because she told me that she borrowed the money to buy it.'

'So that brings us to plan B.'

'Which is?'

'To try to find out how the clock was taken from my mother's cottage. As far as I can remember, it was arranged that a local auctioneer should put the contents of the cottage in his next sale and that was done pretty quickly. Your clock I boxed up separately and labelled it clearly not to be included in the auction. I told the executors about it and they said they would arrange for someone to pick it up. So we had better go and see the auctioneer. One very distinct possibility is that he or one of his employees swapped the two clocks over. They had a key to the property and it would be an easy thing to do. They would probably have a good idea of the value of your clock, and would find it easy to obtain a replacement to swap it with. But it was a bit risky on their part to use a local antique dealer to fence the real thing, if that's the correct expression. The lady dealer and the local auctioneer would be bound to know each other. I suppose it's possible that they are in it together. They would then brazen it out in the event of our trying to persuade her to give it up.'

'Then there's the awful possibility that my clock got somehow mixed up with all the other items in your mother's cottage, perhaps the label fell off or something, and it was quite genuinely sold in auction, and someone equally genuinely bought it. But that doesn't seem likely because I still ended up with a clock of some sort, and the executors didn't think there was any clock in the auction anyway.'

'OK,' continued Andrew, 'So we move on to plan C. There is the estate agent who also had the keys to the place. No doubt he has staff as well. Estate agents usually know the value of things. I have got to see him to find out how the sale of the cottage is going so we talk to him as well. What makes me less confident about any of these plans is that all these people are local firms who have been in business for a long time.'

With each change of topic Daphne found herself thinking along the same lines as her cousin, or talking in the same vein. They changed places in the MG several times, giving Daphne the opportunity to watch him closely as he was driving, or if she was at the wheel, to observe him as he nodded off in the passenger's seat. She felt an affinity towards him that she had not felt to a man before. Although Andrew was much taller, they both had the same slim build. But it was their faces that above all so closely matched: the somewhat arched eyebrows, the fair complexion, the same snub nose and firm chin. Was it this close resemblance that intrigued her? Was there something matching in their genes?

They crossed the border into Scotland, but it was well after dark when they finally reached the now familiar small hotel in Cruff that they had booked into. The following morning they were treated to a hearty breakfast: porridge, stovies, followed by a full Scottish fry-up. Afterwards, they decided to walk round to the antique shop as it was a cold but crisp day.

'I know precisely where it is,' Daphne told Andrew, 'but I'm still not sure exactly what I shall say to that woman. I just hope that my nerve doesn't crack if she attempts to refute our story.'

'Well, of course you can rely on me to back you up,' Andrew reassured her.

They walked along the same bleak street with its granite block buildings, now looking a little less severe in the sunlight. But when they arrived at the shop they were in for a shock. It was completely shuttered up with a notice on the door informing all would-be customers 'Closed for Xmas and the New Year. Re-opening at the beginning of February.' The shutters covered the main plate glass window so that it was impossible to see in.

Daphne and Andrew were nonplussed. Their main plan of campaign had been thwarted at the outset. They stood in front of the shop wondering what they might do next. Then as they walked a few paces along they both simultaneously had the same idea. Next door on one side was a shop selling Scottish specialities; kilts, sporrans, bagpipes and the like. It too was shut down. But on the other side was a similar shop selling woollen items, and it was open.

It was very old-fashioned. On display was a variety of sweaters, jumpers and hats, but its main speciality seemed to be the sale of wool itself. All kinds and colours of wool filled the little shop. Behind the counter sat a middle-aged lady who greeted them with a kindly 'Good morning'. Small and demure, she looked in keeping with her stock-in-trade, several items of which she wore herself, including a hat with a bobble on top.

'I am very sorry to trouble you,' began Daphne.

'Och, I'm sure you're not going to give any trouble,' smiled the little lady in her precise Scottish accent, eager for someone to talk to even if it didn't lead to any business. 'You don't look a troublesome couple.'

'Well,' continued Daphne 'It's really some information I'd like to obtain.'

'If it's local information you require then you've come to the right person. I've lived here for sixty-eight years, so I should have a smattering of knowledge of what's going on in this part of the world.' The lady's eyes twinkled.

'It concerns the antique shop next door,' Daphne explained, 'I was here a week or two ago and I saw something that particularly interested me. I've come back for a second look but I find the shop is closed. We've come all the way from London, so we are very disappointed.'

'If you have come that far to see an item specially, then you would have been well advised to have telephoned beforehand. It would have saved you a wasted journey.'

Daphne suddenly felt very foolish. This little lady was telling her something that should have been obvious, yet neither she nor Andrew had considered that possibility. They had worried about the clock being sold, but not about the shop being shut.

'Most of the business next door, and in many of the shops round here, is to the tourist trade. People don't come here in the depths of winter. I soldier on in my shop because I've got nothing else to do and I live locally. But my neighbour in the shop next door has friends or relatives somewhere where it's warm, so she always shuts down for the winter and goes abroad.'

Daphne and Andrew digested this depressing piece of information. Plucking up courage she asked the lady if she had her neighbour's address or telephone number abroad.

'Yes, I do, as it happens, but I've never managed to get through to her on the phone on the few times I've tried – it's some obscure place in the sun where they don't seem to answer the phone. It's a nuisance because she has given me the keys and I had trouble with the alarm once.'

'You've got the keys to the shop next door?' asked Daphne. There was a pause in the conversation. Andrew looked around the shop: he couldn't see anything he would remotely dream of buying. It all looked like the sort of clothing that was given to him through the International Relief Agency. Even the people of Croatia would balk at this lot, he thought.

'I really would like to see something in the shop next door,' Daphne pleaded. 'I have come a long way. I know I should have telephoned first, but if you're not too busy might you be able to let us into the shop as a very great favour?'

The little lady was about to decline Daphne's request when Andrew stepped into the breach. Picking up the most expensive woollen sweater he could find, he held it up against himself. 'I like the look of this,' he lied. 'How much is it?'

'Eighty-five pounds,' replied the little lady very promptly. 'Pure wool made in Scotland.'

Andrew winced. 'All right. I'll have it. And I'll see if there's anything else I fancy, if, perhaps, while I do so, you would just be kind enough to show my cousin here what she wants to see in the shop next door. That is if you don't mind me being in your shop by myself?'

The little lady was caught out. The uncertainty showed clearly in her face. But the prospect of one if not two sales at this time of the year was too much for her. She gave in.

'Very well,' she conceded, reaching under the counter for a set of keys. 'If you would like to come with me, young lady, I suppose there can't be any harm in it. You will have to wait outside while I unlock the door and deal with the alarm.'

The little lady first found her overcoat, and then beckoned Daphne to follow her next door. 'Just wait outside here,' she told Daphne as she unlocked the door, 'I will have to go inside to unscramble the alarm.' A minute or so later she called Daphne inside.

'Which item was it that you were interested in?'

'I don't see it here.' Daphne's heart was sinking. Had it been sold after all? She looked all round the shop.

'The owner puts some of the more valuable items in a safe in the back room,' the woollen lady told her. She then went to a small kneehole desk in one corner of the shop, pulled open the top drawer on one side, and produced two more keys, while Daphne watched closely. With one key she unlocked a door to the back room and signalled for Daphne to come in. Then she went over to a large safe, fumbled with the keys again, finally managing to get the heavy door open after a fair amount of grumbling. There inside was the clock with the London maker's name on the dial.

'That's it,' cried Daphne excitedly. The two of them lifted the clock out and put it on a table. More than ever Daphne was sure that this was her aunt's clock that should now be rightfully hers.

'I must get in touch with the owner to talk to her about it,' Daphne told the little lady.

'Let's put the clock away and go back to my shop. I can give you the telephone number and address of where she is spending the winter.'

Between the two of them they put the heavy clock back into the safe, and the lady locked the door. They then returned to the main part of the shop, the little lady locked the inner door and returned the keys to the still-open drawer in the desk. 'If you would go back to my shop now, I'll lock up and reset the alarm,' she said.

Back in the wool shop, Andrew completed his purchases with as much good grace as he could manage, while Daphne took a note of the name, telephone number and address of the absent antique dealer. Then they thanked the lady from the wool shop and hurried out.

'Let's go back to the hotel and phone this woman straight away. The address is in Madeira. That can't be too difficult to get through to,' she said.

Back in the hotel they used the phone in Andrew's room to contact Madeira. 'This is going to prove an expensive trip for me,' he complained. But he was wrong. The phone rang and rang but there was no reply.

'She doesn't have to be in all the time. The woollen lady said that she could never get through. We can try again this evening. In the meantime I suggest we try one of our other leads. Let's have a go at the auction room.'

They ordered a pot of coffee in the lounge and found that the auction room was some fifteen minutes' walk away. So as soon as they had refreshed themselves they set off again. It proved to be a very humble place indeed – an old stone-built building on the edge of the village, that might once have been a barn. There were hardly any windows and those that were there were high up and barred.

The two of them pushed open the door and entered a small part of the building that had been partitioned off to form an office. In the barn at the back they could see a collection of farm implements, second-hand furniture and general bric-a-brac, hardly any of which justified the sign outside proclaiming the 'next auction of antiques'. The office itself was cluttered with auction catalogues, notices and odd items that were presumably being catalogued. A young man with horn-rimmed glasses and a somewhat shabby apron stood up from behind a desk and greeted Andrew.

'Mr Fletcher, sir,' he said recognising Andrew. 'I hope you were satisfied with the sale of your late mother's possessions? Have you some more items you wish to dispose of?'

'No, I am afraid not. You sold everything in your last auction, thank you very much. I was very impressed with how speedily it all went through. Do you think I could look at the catalogue for the auction that they were in?'

'Certainly, sir.' The horn-rimmed auctioneer found a copy and passed it over to Andrew. It was not a very substantial document and it did not take Andrew long to see that there were no clocks in it.

'No clocks in that auction, I see?'

'No sir, we mostly get items from farms, and similar agricultural items. That's our speciality and we cover a fairly wide area for that.'

'I did leave one box in my mother's cottage which I asked not to be put in the auction, and clearly marked it accordingly.'

'That's right, sir. I supervised the clearance and cataloguing of your mother's things myself. I remember seeing the box there and I am sure it was still there when we finished our clearance. Is there a problem with it? Can I be of help in any way?' The horn-rimmed auctioneer scented that there might be another object for his sale and he didn't want to miss out.

'I don't think so. It was just that I left this particular box for the executors to collect as it was to be treated separately in my mother's will and I wanted to make sure that they did in fact pick up the clock.' Andrew hadn't meant to say the word 'clock' which slipped out accidentally.

The auctioneer reacted rather nervously to Andrew's comments, shuffling the papers he had in his hand and dropping them on the floor.

'Do I understand you to say that there was a clock in the box, sir? Of course I don't wish to intrude on your private arrangements and really it's no business of mine.'

'Yes, as a matter of fact it was a clock. I was just wanting to make sure that the arrangements were correctly followed through.'

'I don't quite know how to say this, and I hope that it won't upset anybody. And I would ask you not to repeat it to anyone else. But as I did the clearance for you I regard you as a valued customer.' He paused. 'Well to tell the truth, I believe that the box was collected by a local antique dealer – there is only one in the village. I assumed you wished the clock to be sold directly in the trade as I am aware that my auction does not usually deal with items of this nature.' In fact the horn-rimmed one had been decidedly miffed at the fact that he had been given all the lesser items to sell, while it seemed that the antique shop had got the cream. It was a chance for him to put a spoke in the wheel of the lady with the shop and he quite relished the opportunity to put one over on his rival in trade.

'How can you be sure?'

'Well, I can't be sure, as I didn't actually see it collected.

But I do know that at about that time she had a very high quality clock appear in her window, and rumour had it that it came from a local deceased's estate. And you did say the box contained a clock.'

This was indeed news for Andrew and Daphne. At last they seemed to have taken a step forward. The clock, it would appear, had gone directly from Andrew's mother's home to the dealer's shop. How could that be?

'You have been very helpful, Mr . . .' Andrew looked about him hoping to spot the auctioneer's name somewhere, but failed.

'McNeal, sir. Very glad to be of service. Is there anything else I can help you with?' he asked obsequiously, rearranging his papers.

'No, not for the time being, thank you, but we are in the village for a day or two, so if anything further develops perhaps we could call in.'

Andrew and Daphne left the musty ramshackle auction room and its equally ramshackle proprietor. By now it was lunchtime and they decided to try the food in the severe-looking pub just across the road. They ordered the local speciality – venison – and set about discussing the situation.

Andrew began. 'It's clear we must talk to this lady dealer. She's got the clock and she is at the centre of this affair. We can try phoning her again this evening, but I get a feeling we are going to have to see her face-to-face somehow or other. And we don't want to wait until February when she comes back from Madeira.'

'Shall we give the other auctioneer a try this afternoon? We'll have time to kill and I can assure you there's not a lot happening around here in the middle of December,' replied Daphne.

7

After lunch they made their way round to the local estate agents. This time the premises were very modern, or rather they had been substantially modernised. The underlying granite stonework of the building was still there, but numerous neon lights, lit even in the afternoon, and a variety of signs, billboards and posters served to give the place an up-to-date look.

They entered the neatly-furnished office with its modern equipment and were greeted by an efficient-looking young man in a suit and tie. He recognised Andrew immediately, and after being introduced to Daphne, offered them both a seat. Straight away he launched into a sales patter that he obviously had often used before.

'I expect you have come to hear how we are getting on with the sale of your mother's property?' he enquired, but without waiting for a reply, continued. 'As you see from our window we have had the cottage photographed and circulated to our clients. We have managed to create considerable interest and have already shown four clients around the property.' He went on in considerable detail to expound on how well he was progressing, but the fact of the matter was that he had not yet had an offer.

Andrew was not really surprised. After all, the demand for rural properties in some need of repair in this part of Scotland was bound to be limited. However, the estate agent was getting into his stride, impressing Andrew on the range of clients at his disposal, the mortgage facilities he could arrange for any would-be purchaser and the likelihood that before long his firm would be receiving an offer which he would immediately be conveying to the solicitors who were handling the estate. When finally the young man's spiel seemed to be running out of steam Andrew enquired blandly whether he was the only person in the business or whether he had any staff. Slightly nonplussed, the estate agent told him that there was also his wife who was very diligent, and excellent at handling the gentlemen customers, while the office was run by his secretary.

'The clearance of the contents went ahead very quickly, didn't it?' enquired Andrew, 'So I suppose you put the cottage on the market soon after that?'

'That's right. Mr McNeal the auctioneer had an auction coming up just at the right time and it all seemed to go ahead very smoothly.'

'Yes,' said Andrew, 'Once my mother had died I didn't like to stay in the cottage for any length of time. I left it to the executors, the auctioneers and you to deal with matters. You didn't by any chance notice a box that I had labelled not to go in the auction?'

'I did the measuring up myself after the contents were cleared, and I did see that box, as I had to make a thorough inspection of the premises. I . . .' He was about to launch into another lengthy disquisition on how he had measured everything when Andrew interrupted him.

'Do you know what happened to the box?'

'All I know is that it was definitely there when I was measuring and photographing, but I am sure it had gone when I brought the first client round. I assumed the executors had taken it as instructed on the box.'

'Were there any photos of the interior?'

'No, I'm afraid not. We just concentrated on the exterior and the delightful setting.'

'At this stage both Daphne and Andrew decided that they were not going to glean any more information from this source, but were in danger of being on the receiving end of another splurge of sales rhetoric, so they took their leave.

'I never really thought it might be him,' said Daphne, and Andrew agreed. 'But of course he might be lying. You never know.'

They made their way back to the hotel and ordered a pot of tea. The estate agent had been so loquacious that it was already four o'clock and getting dark.

'Let's have another go at Madeira now,' said Daphne. 'I'm pretty sure they are an hour ahead of us. We might be lucky this time.'

They went upstairs to Andrew's room to telephone. This time they did get through. A woman's voice answered in what Daphne assumed must be Portuguese. Daphne was nonplussed. Italian she could cope with, but Portuguese was a different matter. 'Do you speak English?' she enquired. Whatever the reply was it came in Portuguese. Then a further few sentences in Portuguese and the phone clicked silent.

'What a bore,' groaned Daphne.

They went back to the lounge and sat round the large log fire, treating themselves to a Scotch each in an attempt to revive their spirits. They decided to leave it to the evening before they tried to get through again, hoping that the antique dealer was not too much of a night owl.

As they sat down to dinner together that evening in the small but cosy dining room, Daphne listened with interest to Andrew's talk of his missions in different parts of the world. 'It's not well paid, but it is stimulating, varied and satisfying. I never know where I am going next.' As he spoke Daphne felt the last vestiges of any doubt that he might be the guilty party disappearing, to be replaced by feelings of an altogether different nature. He was certainly a very likeable man and she couldn't think of anyone she would more like to have dinner with on a cold December evening in Scotland.

The conversation veered back to the events of the day. 'Well, did you like your clock?' Andrew asked. Daphne started to picture the clock and the shop it was in when suddenly she put down her knife and fork.

'I've just had a brilliant idea,' she told her cousin. 'Unless she actually stole the clock herself, the lady from the antique shop must have paid out an awful lot of money for it. She's hardly likely to have paid in cash an amount of that size. She would have paid by cheque – she told me she got a bank loan – and probably got a receipt. The woollen lady took the keys out of a desk to unlock the safe and I noticed that there were some bank books in the drawer. Although the inner room was locked, the desk itself was not. If I could get a look at the cheque book I should be able to see on the stub who the cheque was paid to. There might even be a receipt there.'

'That would be a big step forward. How are we going to do that?

'We are obviously going to have to persuade the woollen lady to let us into the antique shop again.'

'I don't like the sound of that. This trip is already running away with my inheritance. I've got a feeling I'm going to see some more of it disappear tomorrow.'

'Don't be stingy, Andrew. This is what we will do. You ask to see the clock in the inner room. I'll come into the shop with you. While you and the woollen lady are in the inner room I'll look in the drawer with the bank stuff.'

'OK. At least I get to see the clock again. I can then be sure in my own mind that it is indeed the same clock my mother owned. I'm sure I'd recognise it, as I packed it up only a few weeks ago. If it ever gets to a court of law and I have to swear it's my mother's clock, as I am beginning to feel that's the way all this is going, then at least I'll be sure of my facts.'

They completed their meal, tried unsuccesfully to get through to Madeira again, and made their way up to their rooms. On the spur of the moment Daphne kissed Andrew goodnight on the cheek. When it looked as if he might return the kiss more positively, Daphne slipped quickly into her room, not sufficiently sure of her emotions to allow things to progress too rapidly.

The following morning they enjoyed another hearty Scottish breakfast together. Daphne was beginning to fear that any weight she had lost from her trip to Croatia was about to be put back on again in Scotland. She was also conscious that the small case she had brought meant that she was going to be wearing the same clothes for a period of days. She remarked on this to Andrew.

'Never mind,' he comforted her. 'It looks as if I shall be making up in the fashion scene for whatever you lack – unless you would like to choose something in the woollen shop? And that reminds me – I'll have to get some more cash from the bank first.'

They set off after breakfast. Cruff boasted both a bank and a building society. Andrew drew some more cash from the bank and the two of them went round to the wool shop just as the owner was opening up.

She was clearly delighted to see the couple again, and ushered them in. The two women exchanged pleasantries while Andrew cast despairingly round for something that wasn't too antiquated.

'Look, Andrew,' Daphne said, 'There's a pair of tartan trews there that would go so well with what you bought yesterday. Hold them up against you to see if they fit.'

Andrew took the trousers off the peg to hold them up against himself. They were no more than an inch too short. He looked at the waist size. At least that was right.

'You must get them,' Daphne told him turning to the shopkeeper who was beaming widely and nodding approval at Andrew's choice.

'My cousin would like to look at the clock in the shop next door as he didn't get a chance to see it yesterday. Would it be an awful imposition to ask you to take us next door as you did yesterday so that he can help me make up my mind? I expect he will buy something else when we get back in your shop.'

The little Scottish lady realised she had been put on the spot. Having given in yesterday she could scarcely say no to-day.

'Aye. I'll take you both in then. Just let me get my coat and the keys.' Andrew and Daphne followed the lady out of her shop. They waited while she unlocked the antique shop and went inside to unscramble the alarm. Then they both went into the shop while the lady walked over to the desk, opened the drawer and took out the keys to the inner room and the safe.

73

'I'll stay in this room as there's not much space in the inner room,' Daphne told the lady. The other two then went into the back room. Daphne heard the lady start to unlock the safe.

Seizing her chance while she was briefly alone in the main room she moved smartly over to the desk with the drawer still open and took out the cheque book. Quickly she flipped back the latest cheque stubb. It read 'M. Thompson £100'. The next read 'T. Newsam £1000.' She turned it over to come to the next one, and then gasped in amazement at what was written on it. 'Mildred Fletcher £20,000.' The cheque was made out to a dead person – Andrew's mother! Hurriedly she returned the cheque book to the drawer to wait in great excitement for Andrew to finish his examination of the clock. She heard the safe door shut and they both came back into the main room.

'Super clock,' Andrew said. 'I think that should definitely be yours, Daphne.'

The Scottish lady locked up everything and they all trooped back to her shop. Andrew duly bought the plaid trews and added a Scottish bonnet with a bobble to his ensemble.

'All wool,' smiled the shopkeeper as she rang up the till. 'Goodbye, my dears.'

Daphne could scarcely contain herself until they were outside the shop. 'The cheque was made out to your mother for £20,000,' she told Andrew. 'How can that possibly be?' Andrew was equally dumbfounded. They decided to repeat yesterday's itinerary and discussed the surprising revelation over a cup of coffee.

'Firstly, it must be the cheque to buy the clock,' Daphne told Andrew when they were seated. 'The lady told me she had to borrow the money from the bank. Is it possible that your mother agreed to sell the clock before she died, but the antique dealer didn't actually collect it until after her death?' Daphne asked as they digested both the coffee and the latest development.

'That hardly seems likely. I suppose my mother could have

74

sold it but surely she would have told me and altered the will. What was the date on the cheque? If it was before my mother's death I suppose it is just possible my mother did agree to sell it and it was collected later, in which case all our efforts of the last couple of weeks have been wasted and I've got a collection of Scottish clothes I need never have had!'

Daphne was silent for a while. 'I never thought to look at the date,' she admitted.

'Oh dear,' groaned Andrew, 'don't tell me I've got to add some more plaids to my wardrobe.'

'I'm afraid so – we'll just have to go back to find out the date on the cheque. But as it's my fault I didn't notice the date, I'll be the one to bribe our woollen lady. I'll buy a sweater to match yours and people will hardly be able to tell us apart! And I've got a horrible feeling that we aren't going to be able to squeeze all these extra clothes into the MG anyway.'

They finished their coffees and walked smartly back to the all-too-familiar woollen shop. The sun had come out making the air seem positively crisp. When they reached it the shop window was bathed in sunlight making the brightly coloured plaids look unexpectedly attractive. 'Perhaps this won't be such a waste of money after all,' thought Daphne eyeing one of the more luridly decorated sweaters through the window.

The woollen lady was clearly pleased to see them when they came into her shop again.

'Hullo, my dears, what can I do for you this time?'

'I won't beat about the bush,' Daphne told her honestly. 'My cousin would like to see the clock next door again and I'm going to bribe you by buying one of those sweaters there.' She picked up two or three until she was satisfied she had one that would fit her and bought it on the spot, handing the money to the lady who was already reaching down under her counter for the keys, a resigned but not discontented look on her face.

The three of them went through the same rigmarole with which each was now familiar. While Andrew and the shopkeeper were in the inner room examining the clock, Daphne slipped over to the desk, took out the chequebook and looked at the date on the cheque stub – 10 November 1996. Quickly she replaced the chequebook and waited for the other two to return to the main room. Finally the alarm was set, everything was locked up and they returned to the bright sunlight outside.

'I shall have to order some more stock if you need to inspect that clock again,' the woollen lady remarked with a wistful smile. 'Goodbye my dears – if you do buy that clock you will need a few more pennies than you have spent in my shop.'

They waved goodbye. As soon as she was out of earshot Daphne told Andrew the date on the cheque.

'So, my mother died on October 10th. The cheque was made out to a dead person. I don't understand it. What good would it be to anybody?'

'We have to speak to the antiques lady. She will surely be able to explain what has been going on. Let's go back to the hotel and see if we can get through again, although even if we do this hardly seems a matter to discuss over the telephone, particularly when she stands to lose £20,000.'

'Yes, I don't think we can really put this to her over the phone. She doesn't know who we are, and it would be difficult enough face to face, but at least then we could show her some sort of documentary evidence in support. We would even have our passports to show who we are, plus my mother's will and the letter from the executors saying you had inherited the clock. I think we must visit the executors to get a copy of their letter to you, and I'll ask for a copy of the will.'

'So, assuming we get through to Madeira, are you prepared to fly out there with me?' Daphne asked.

'Well, I've come so far I might as well spend a bit more of my inheritance. At least Madeira should be warmer than either Scotland or Croatia and it's a place I haven't been to before.'

When they arrived back at the hotel they went up to Andrew's room where Daphne dialled the number in

Madeira again. This time the voice at the other end spoke in English with a Scottish accent.

'Is that Mrs Campbell?' Daphne asked.

'I am.'

'I came into your shop before you went away and saw an antique bracket clock there; you may remember me?'

'Aye, I do that.'

'I would like to talk to you about it, but it's rather difficult over the telephone. I'm prepared to come out to see you in Madeira if that would be convenient for you?'

Sensing a possible sale of an expensive piece, Mrs Campbell was only too willing to accommodate her enquirer.

'That's fine,' she assured her. 'I shall be here for a month or more, and although I go out most days I'm usually back by the late evening. Do you have my address here?'

'Yes, the lady in the wool shop next door gave it to me with your telephone number. I shall fly out as soon as I can make the arrangements at this end, and phone you at the end of the day for an appointment when I arrive, which I hope will be in a couple of days.'

'I look forward to meeting you. Goodbye.'

Turning to Andrew Daphne said, 'That's another encouraging step forward. Now it's your turn to get in touch with the executor.'

It didn't take long to find the executor's number. Andrew asked the receptionist if he could speak to the person dealing with his mother's estate.

'I'm Mr Drury,' said a voice at the other end of the line. 'I'm afraid Mr Sergeant, who is dealing with your mother's estate, is not here at present.'

'I really only want a copy of the will and of a letter to my cousin.'

'That doesn't sound too difficult. Come round now and I'll arrange it.'

8

They duly presented themselves at the solicitor's and were ushered into the presence of Mr Drury, a portly gentleman of about sixty, with glasses and old-fashioned side-whiskers. He was dressed in a dark suit and tie.

'I must apologise for my partner's absence,' he said, 'but he is away with the flu. However, I have your documents, Mr Fletcher, and my secretary will have them photographed for you. I've taken the opportunity to look briefly at your file and things seem to be progressing satisfactorily. I see that probate was obtained quite quickly, that the contents of the property have been sold, and that a progress payment has been made. I see also that the one bequest in the will to you, Miss Fleet, has been handed over.' Daphne nodded in agreement.

'We now have to await the sale of the property. Inevitably that will take longer, but we will inform you as soon as we have some positive news.'

'I'd like to give you a more permanent address,' Andrew said, 'I was only briefly in Malta. It would be better if you write to me at this address in Rome.' He gave the solicitor the address of the flat in Rome that Daphne had taken so long to trace.

'You are clearly a man on the move,' the solicitor commented. 'I've spent my whole life here in Cruff and never felt the need to wander overseas.'

The secretary brought in the copies they had asked for. As there didn't seem to be anything further they could do at the solicitor's office the two of them returned to their hotel.

'I can't see that there's anything to keep us here now. We might as well return to London. I'd feel happier trying to book a couple of air tickets to Madeira down there,' Andrew said. Daphne agreed and phoned her mother to warn her they would both be returning to Fulham.

Once again they clambered into the MG. This time the problem of squeezing the luggage in was even more difficult, as a result of their visits to the woollen shop. After a tiring journey they were not sorry to be back in Fulham where Andrew spent the night in the spare room.

The following day they were lucky to be able to buy two tickets to Madeira for the next day. Daphne rearranged her wardrobe, throwing out all the sweaters and jeans she had worn in Scotland, and packing instead some lighter summery outfits. Andrew was not so lucky – he certainly did not want to take what he had bought in Scotland, but he had only a limited range of clothes with him. 'Perhaps I can find the Madeira equivalent of the woollen shop when we get out there,' he remarked, 'and then I can kit up with something more appropriate.'

Before they left London they phoned Mrs Campbell in Madeira to let her know when they would be arriving. This time they left calling late enough to be sure she was at home. She undertook to meet them at the airport and take them to a hotel.

The landing next day at Madeira was quite stimulating as the runway seemed to be built on the very edge of the sea. They passed through the customs and baggage retrieval hall without problem and passed out into the warm Madeira air. They looked around the various people assembled to meet the plane, but Daphne could not identify Mrs Campbell. However, a very smart healthy-looking woman dressed in a bright pair of yellow shorts and a T-shirt with dolphins leaping all over it came forward to greet her with a big smile. 'Welcome to Madeira,' she said, 'I hope you had a pleasant flight, Miss Fleet.'

With a shock that she failed to conceal in her expression Daphne now recognised the tweedy lady she had first met on a freezing day in Scotland. 'Mrs Campbell?' she queried, 'I'm delighted to see you. I admit I didn't recognise you at first – you have certainly acclimatised yourself very well. What a difference from the last time we met only a short while ago.'

'I've found you a pleasant hotel in the centre of Funchal, the capital,' Mrs Campbell told them. 'It won't take long on the new roads they have built here.'

The drive was a delight along a dramatic new highway, and Funchal proved to be a city of trees and flowers. They could easily understand what attracted Mrs Campbell away from her shop in Scotland, as she described at some length the various delights of the island that occupied her days there.

'Would it be convenient for you if we could talk to you right away?' Daphne asked. 'We have something urgent to ask you.'

'OK,' Mrs Campbell agreed. 'I'll find a nice restaurant in the old town. Do you like fish? They have a speciality here called escapado, fished out of the deeps of the Atlantic.'

The three of them were shortly seated in a small restaurant near the harbour within smelling distance of the sea and the fish market. When they had ordered their fish, Mrs Campbell, who was beginning to realise that this was to be no ordinary sale, asked, 'So, my dears, what's this all about?'

'It's about the very expensive bracket clock you have in your shop, Mrs Campbell,' Daphne began. 'I'm afraid that what we have to say will not come as very good news to you.'

'You mean you haven't come all this way to make me an offer?'

'First let me tell you who we are. Andrew here is my cousin.

80

His mother died quite recently in Scotland. There was a will in which Andrew was the main beneficiary, but in the estate there was a clock that was left to me. I went to Scotland at the time I first met you to collect that clock from the solicitors who are handling the will for Andrew. However, the clock that the solicitors gave me is not, we are sure, the one that belonged to Andrew's mother. Then, when I saw the clock in your shop window I recognised it as the one my aunt had, particularly after it played the music. We realise that this must come as a nasty shock for you, but we have brought with us some papers to substantiate what we have been saying. We have both a copy of the will and of the executor's letter telling me of my inheritance. We also have our passports to prove our identities.'

Daphne then produced all these documents for Mrs Campbell's inspection. She was clearly taken aback. Far from arranging the sale of the clock, she was now in a very difficult position.

'You had better hear my story,' she said. 'Cruff is a very small place and when I heard of your mother's death, Mr Fletcher, I did something I probably should not have. I contacted the estate agent. There is only one in Cruff. I asked if he would mind if I saw the property when he was measuring it up for sale. You see, I knew your mother and I had visited her once or twice, Mr Fletcher. I had seen the clock then and knew it was valuable, even if your mother did not. When I saw the clock in the box at the time the estate agent was measuring the cottage after the rest of the contents had been sold I decided to contact the solicitors, who were the only ones in the village, to see if they were dealing with the estate. When I found out that they were, I expressed an interest in the clock if it was going to be sold. Not so long after I received a call from them to tell me the clock was indeed going to be sold. After some haggling we negotiated a price, I secured a loan from the bank and duly bought the clock. The funny thing is

I never actually met anyone from the solicitor's office. They just told me to send them a cheque for the agreed amount and then I could collect the clock directly from Mrs Fletcher's cottage, which I did.'

'And to whom did you make the cheque payable?'

'To your late mother, Mr Fletcher. The solicitor told me it would be part of the estate and that seemed natural enough to me. I believe I have a legal title to the clock as I bought it from the estate, paid by cheque, and as far as I know everything is above board. Obviously I have not seen the will and had no idea that it had been willed to you, Miss Fleet. I'm not sure what the position is in these circumstances, but I presume that there has been some terrible mistake in dealing with the estate. But I want to emphasise that as far as I'm concerned I acted in good faith and was totally unaware of the situation with the will. However, I can see we have a problem here, and I'm most anxious that we should arrive at a satisfactory solution. I have been trading for a long while in Cruff, and have built up a good reputation which I wouldn't wish to have tarnished. I don't understand how this situation has come about, but I can see that it is important to have it resolved as soon as possible. I would mention that the clock was of considerably more value than the type of things I usually trade in, and any problems would place me in difficulty.'

During lunch, the three of them went over the events several times without being able to throw any more light on what might have happened. Mrs Campbell was obviously becoming increasingly concerned at this unexpected turn of events.

'I presume you will now go back to the executors to find out what has happened?' she queried. 'I think I had better come back with you. This is too important an amount of money for me to be able to take lightly, and I shall be worrying about it all over Christmas. If that is agreeable to you and you don't mind me going with you, I'd like to get the matter cleared up quickly.'

Daphne and Andrew agreed with their worried host and were as perplexed as she was over this latest development. As the three of them finished their meal they agreed that they would all return to Britain as soon as possible. Mrs Campbell offered to telephone either the airport or a local travel agent to secure three seats on a plane back to Britain.

'In view of what has happened, I will pay the bill,' Andrew offered.

'And I will ferry you to your hotel and telephone you as soon as I have news on the flights,' Mrs Campbell offered in return.

The hotel was not far away, built on a cliff overlooking Funchal and the bay. They checked in, said goodbye to Mrs Campbell and went out on the terrace to admire the view.

'We might as well make the most of this while we can,' Andrew said. 'It doesn't look as if our stay is going to be a lengthy one.'

Sure enough, they received a phone call from Mrs Campbell only an hour later to tell them that she had reserved three seats on a plane back to the UK the next day, and that they should all meet up at the airport in time to catch the plane.

The following morning they spent meandering among the tree-lined streets and squares of Funchal before packing up again to get a taxi to take them back to the airport. When they were finally seated on the plane together they made their plans for the return to Scotland.

'We shall stay overnight in London at my mother's house in Fulham. I'm afraid we can't offer to put you up, Mrs Campbell, as we don't have enough bedrooms,' Daphne said.

'Never mind, I'll go straight back to Scotland. I'll leave you my home phone number so that you can let me know as soon as you have some news. I think I ought to see my solicitor to find out what advice he can give me. It should be quite interesting as he is the same firm as yours. Not surprising, I suppose, as there is only the one in the village.

'Then we can all meet together at the solicitors. This time I will make sure we have an appointment. I seem to be spending my life chasing after people just recently.'

9

Two days later all three were assembled in the rather cramped confines of the solicitor's office, with its pictures of highland scenes vying for space on the walls with fading photos of the founding partners of the practice. The highland stags, the sheep and the original partners all seemed to be looking down on the present incumbents with the same haughty, disapproving stare.

Mr Drury, the senior partner, sat behind a desk piled high with files and papers. He was dressed in the same sombre suit he had previously been wearing, totally in keeping with his surroundings. One could imagine the doughty sheep in the pictures on the wall supplying the wool for his worsted suit at the time when the pictures had been painted. Mrs Campbell was back in tweeds and brogues while Daphne and Andrew wore the sweaters they had previously bought in the village.

Mr Drury opened the conversation after bidding them good morning and supplying them with coffee and oatmeal biscuits. 'I understand from Mr Fletcher that all three of you wish to see me regarding the late Mrs Fletcher's will.' The three of them nodded agreement.

'I also understand, Mrs Campbell, that although you are not a beneficiary in the will, you are in some way involved and that this may lead you to seeking my advice.' Again Mrs Campbell nodded.

'Let me say first of all that my junior partner, Mr Sergeant, who is dealing with this case, is still away. As far as I know there has been no further progress with the will since your last visit, Mr Fletcher. I have the file in front of me now; can you let me know how I can help you?'

Daphne then explained about the clock, and Mrs Campbell in turn told him her story.

'That certainly is very strange,' Mr Drury admitted. 'The person you spoke to, Mrs Campbell, must have been Mr Sergeant, because it wasn't me and there are just the two of us here. If a cheque was issued by you to the late Mrs Fletcher then it must have been passed through the executor's account at the bank. The bank statement will be in the file here – let's have a look.'

He opened the file and thumbed through the contents, spreading them out over his already cluttered desk.

'Here's the will,' Mr Drury muttered, half to himself. 'The death certificate, the list of assets and liabilities, the probate, ah, and here's the bank statement. Let's see ... here's the proceeds of the sale of the contents of the property coming in, and here's a cheque issued to you for almost the same amount, Mr Fletcher, less the probate fee and one or two late bills. There's also a note that the clock willed to you was handed over in person, Miss Fleet, with your signature in receipt. That seems to be all in order, although you now claim that the clock is the wrong one. The most significant item in the estate, the property, has yet to be sold. But there is no cheque here for £20,000 from you, Mrs Campbell; it hasn't passed through the account. Just a minute, I'll make sure it isn't here awaiting to be paid in.' His podgy hands sifted through the relatively few papers in the file, spreading them out over the desk as he did so.

The three on the other side of the desk watched his movements closely, especially Mrs Campbell, who was becoming increasingly agitated.

'No, there's no cheque here,' Mr Drury announced.

'I can't understand this,' Mrs Campbell said, her face now wearing a worried expression far removed from the happy smile she had first greeted Daphne with in Madeira. 'I've checked my own bank statement and the cheque has been paid. I sent it to this office with a covering letter.'

Mr Drury looked at the file again. 'There's no letter from you here, Mrs Campbell,' he announced in as sympathetic voice as he could manage, mindful that she too was a client of his. 'I am unable to explain the circumstances surrounding either the clock or the cheque, but to judge from the file I cannot see anything that is out of order. Indeed, the winding up of the estate has proceeded very quickly with only the house sale still outstanding. I haven't been able to contact Mr Sergeant who has been away quite a few days now. I left a message for him to phone in yesterday when I knew you were coming in, but I haven't heard from him. He lives locally and I will call on him on my way home this evening. Tomorrow is Saturday. I come in on Saturday mornings. If you would like to telephone me I might have some news for you then, if I have been able to see my partner.'

The four of them were discussing the matter for a few minutes without getting any further. The windows of the cramped, overheated office were steaming up from the extra warmth of the four bodies inside. Mr Drury peered over the top of his glasses at Mrs Campbell, whose expression was now starting to match the foreboding gloom of the faces in the pictures on the wall. 'I shouldn't worry too much, Mrs Campbell,' he said reassuringly. 'I'm sure there must be a logical explanation of this, that will emerge as soon as I can contact my partner.'

The three of them gathered their winter coats and trooped out of the stuffy office to face the cold winter air. 'Come on, Mrs Campbell,' said Andrew still clutching his briefcase of papers he had accumulated, 'I'll buy you a coffee, or something stronger if you wish.'

87

Mrs Campbell accepted gratefully as they walked round to the little teashop where they were the only customers that cold morning.

'You know, I have somehow got the feeling that there was something missing in my mother's file, but I just can't for the life of me think what it is,' Andrew said musingly, sipping his coffee. 'We could see all the papers and documents spread out over Mr Drury's desk, and he twice went through the file.' He gazed vacantly out of the window at the sombre stone building society opposite. Suddenly his eyes lit up.

'Got it,' he cried, pointing to the drab building on the other side of the street. The two women looked out of the window and then at Andrew in some amazement.

'What on earth can be in there?' Mrs Campbell asked, her face still in the forlorn-sheep mode it had adopted in the solicitor's office.

'The building society,' Andrew announced, 'that's what's missing.' The other two looked at him confused.

'My mother kept an account at the building society. She always had the book on the dresser with her pension book and she used to go in there every week. When she died I not only received the money from the sale of the contents shortly afterwards, I also received the balance on her building society account – about £6,000. But there was no building society book in the file. I am sure I would have noticed, and Mr Drury, who read out to us all the things in the file, didn't mention it. Also, neither the money from the building society account nor the payment to me of the outstanding balance showed in the executors' bank statement. So where is it? I'm sure that any methodical professional person would not have thrown away the book, certainly not before the estate was finally wound up. And in any case the documents should rightfully belong to me.'

A slight glimmer of hope filtered across Mrs Campbell's sad sheep-like face. 'Do you think we could go into the building society to find out?' she ventured. 'Although I can't see that it would help much. I keep an account there. But it's worth a try, isn't it?' Suddenly she was becoming more positive; the sheep giving way to the stag in her expression.

The three of them hurriedly finished their coffee and walked across the road to the building society, where they asked to see the manager. She appeared dressed in a smart green uniform that somehow seemed slightly smarter than the similar green uniforms worn by the two cashiers in the front office. She immediately recognised Mrs Campbell as a customer. After a brief introduction Andrew explained why they were there.

'I can't possibly supply you with any information about another customer's account, Mr Fletcher, even if it is of your late mother,' she told them. 'I assume the account is now closed and we would have paid the balance to the executors or his agent on sight of probate and the death certificate. I will just look at the account because I do remember something about it. Will you excuse me while I go to the other office to look at the computer screen?'

She disappeared for a few minutes and returned with a computer print-out and a thoughtful look on her face.

'Yes, I do remember now how this account was closed. Did you say you are the son of the late Mrs Fletcher, and also the main beneficiary in the will?' Andrew nodded in assent.

'You don't by any chance have proof of identity do you?'

Andrew unzipped his briefcase. 'Here is my passport as proof of identity. And here is a copy of the will showing me as the main beneficiary. I don't have a copy of probate but I can easily get it.' Andrew was pleased that he had kept all his papers with him.

'We have already seen the probate and the death certificate, following which we paid out the balance on the account to Messrs Smith and Drury, the executors. We did however have a special request from the solicitors regarding this account. I'm going to phone them to get their authority to show you this print-out. Can you bear with me while I do so?' The three visitors agreed, and the manager rang the solicitors. Permission was granted quite readily. She continued talking. 'Normally we close an account as soon as we get notification of death. Sometimes there is an odd dividend cheque or something similar which comes through after death, and it may be that we don't hear about the death until quite a while after the actual date of death, so that standing orders, dividends and such go through the account after the date of death. But in this case we knew very quickly. As I have said we paid out the balance to the executors, but they came to see me at about that time with another cheque which they said had come in late and asked if they could pass it through the account. The cheque was payable to the late Mrs Fletcher and strictly speaking I suppose it should have been returned or perhaps passed through the executors account, but as it happened so soon after death, I agreed the transaction – it was just a formality and would have gone through anyway if we hadn't heard of the death so quickly.'

She passed the computer print-out over to the three visitors. There on one side of the account was a payment in for £20,000, and on the other side dated a few days later, a withdrawal of the same amount.

'There you are, you see,' repeated the manager, 'pure formality.'

The effect on the other three was far from a formality. My cheque,' cried Mrs Campbell, her face lighting up.

'Who was it at the solicitors that you dealt with?' Andrew asked.

'Well, it wasn't Mr Drury, I've just been speaking to him and I know him quite well. It was his younger partner, a quite large gentleman, dark, with glasses. I can't remember his name nor do I think that I had seen him before, but all his paperwork was in order, or we wouldn't have dealt with it as we did. I can sense that there is some sort of a problem here – can I help in an way?'

'You've been extremely helpful already,' Daphne told her. 'At long last it looks as if we are beginning to understand something that has been a considerable mystery to us. There is one other question I should like to ask, however. Could the withdrawal have been in cash?'

'It would be quite exceptional for a sum of that size to be paid in cash and could be done only with prior notice. But I can tell from this computer print-out that it was as usual made by cheque.'

'And who would the cheque be payable to?'

'The solicitors, I suppose.'

'Can we keep this computer print-out?'

'Well, I may have already stepped over the traces rather more than I should, so I will say no to that request. But I will deliver it to the executors and they can pass it over to you if they wish.'

The three of them conferred together. 'We propose to go back to see Mr Drury now if he is free. Could we take it with us?'

'I will come round with you,' the manager said obligingly. 'Just let me give Mr Drury another ring to make sure he is available.'

She made the necessary phone call. 'He will see us in a quarter of an hour. If we walk round slowly we should be in time.'

10

The snow had begun to fall again as the four of them made their way to the solicitor's office. The manager was obviously inquisitive to know what this was all about, but her training and many years' service in the building society prevented her from asking an outright question. Daphne told her that it was a matter of interpreting a will, where the building society passbook had been mislaid, and that seemed to satisfy her. They were quite cold by the time they arrived back at the solicitor's office. The four of them were shown into Mr Drury's confined room.

'I have something for you, Mr Drury,' the manager said, passing the envelope with the computer print-out over to him. 'It's a print-out of an account of Mr Fletcher's late mother. I understand the passbook has been mislaid. I thought it best to give it to you as executor, so that you can deal with it as you see fit.'

Mr Drury thanked her and she took her leave. With one less in the room, they were all able to sit down again. The faces in the pictures on the wall looked as gloomily haughty as before, but those of the three visitors had a more expectant air.

'It suddenly occurred to me that the building society passbook was missing from the file – I have already received the balance on the account at the same time as the proceeds of the sale of the contents of the cottage. I thought it might be helpful in tracing Mrs Campbell's missing cheque if you were to see a print-out of the book,' Andrew told the solicitor.

'Aye, but...' began the venerable solicitor, opening the envelope and reading its contents. He stopped in mid-sentence as his eyes lighted on the two £20,000 transactions. He frowned, looked at the statement for a full minute in silence and then began to fold it up again.

'I have to tell you that we are aware of the contents of the statement, Mr Drury,' Daphne told him.

'I see,' he replied, 'I'm not sure what to make of this. Strictly speaking, all transactions after death should pass through the executors' account which we have opened at the bank. I can't at the moment see why Mr Sergeant should have wanted to pass that particular cheque through the building society.'

'But it does show that my cheque for £20,000 was received, that I did buy the clock and therefore came by it legally,' Mrs Campbell piped in.

'There is certainly a transaction for £20,000 going through the books,' admitted Mr Drury.

'But where is the money now?' she asked, her face brightening as Mr Drury's frown deepened.

'And how is it that my clock was sold at all?' added Daphne.

'It looks as if I had better pay Mr Sergeant a visit more urgently than I originally anticipated. It's coming up to lunchtime, now – I don't have an appointment for lunch, so I think I will visit him straight away.'

'Perhaps we could come with you? Daphne asked. 'After all, we are all directly involved in this, and we have come a long way to try to resolve the matter.'

Somewhat reluctantly the solicitor agreed. 'I'll just check his address, but I know he lives in digs on the outskirts of the village. He hasn't been answering his phone, but he should be in bed if he has the flu as he says he has. His landlady may know where he is if he is not in.' Mr Drury checked the address. 'If you would like to come with me, then. It's not far and my car is just round the corner.'

They all trooped out of the tiny office which had again become stiflingly hot with so many bodies in such a small space. Their departure was watched impassively by the silent faces on the walls.

The snow was beginning to lie again as the four of them clambered into Mr Drury's small saloon. 'I haven't got a family and I don't travel much outside the locality, unlike you, Mr Fletcher, so I don't need a large car. And, of course, as a Scotsman I mind it's more economical,' he told his passengers. There was a brief lull in the conversation as they set off. Daphne was the first to break the silence.

'I think at long last I am beginning to understand what's going on here. I knew as soon as I saw it that the clock I received from Mr Sergeant was not the one my aunt taught me to tell the time on. Then, by chance, wandering around the village, I saw what I was convinced was my clock in the window of Mrs Campbell's shop, and I also saw from the price label that it was very valuable. At first, I assumed that Andrew, whom I hadn't seen since he was a boy, had switched the clocks over. I spent a considerable amount of time and money tracking him down, but when I finally did find him I began to realise that he wasn't the guilty party, although it took me a while to come to this conclusion. I apologise to you, Andrew.

'Our suspicions – I say our because Andrew and I were now of the same mind – then turned to you, Mrs Campbell. You'll forgive us, I hope, but the circumstances seemed to imply that you were now the guilty party, or at least that you had a hand in dealing with the clock. Now that we've seen the building society account with your cheque passing through it I can see that you have been acting in good faith. So I must apologise to you too.

94

'That brings us to Mr Sergeant. Having been wrong twice already, I'm still not one hundred per cent sure he is responsible, but it would seem that he has some explaining to do at the very least.

'Since it took some time to locate me, he must have realised I was something of a distant relative, out of contact with Andrew's mother, and would probably not be able to remember what the clock looked like. Yet he did trace me, and that must have taken some effort on his part. Assuming that Mr Sergeant is the villain, then for his plan to work it was essential for him to find me. Otherwise, I suppose, the clock would pass to Andrew who would certainly be expected to recognise it, since he packed it up.

'Then he had to dispose of it. That was easy. He sold it, as executor to someone who already knew the value of the clock, who knew that my aunt had died and who had already been enquiring about it. Who knows, it may have been your enquiry, Mrs Campbell, that put the idea in his mind in the first place. You had absolutely no reason to doubt that he was within his rights in selling it.

'The business with the cheque was clever. If he had asked you to make it payable to him as executor he would have had to pass it through the books. Payable to him personally might have looked suspicious.

'He must have been a bit on edge when he actually handed the wrong clock over to me in his office, although I didn't notice it. I almost said something at the time. I wonder what he would have done if I had. By then he had already sold my clock to you, Mrs Campbell, and it was sitting in your shop window. I wonder what he thought each time he saw it there?'

Mr Drury listened intently to Daphne's indictment of his junior partner, the concentrated frown on his face reflecting both the reaction to what Daphne had been saying, and his need to drive through the thickening snow. They had driven a short distance along the road leading away from the village when Mr Drury pulled up outside a large detached house built of the usual granite blocks.

'Here we are,' he said, 'I think it best if I talk to him alone first. Despite what you say, Miss Fleet, there may be a perfectly logical explanation of all this. Even a solicitor is innocent until proved guilty.'

He switched off the engine and ponderously climbed out of the car. Even more laboriously he mounted the steep steps up to the front of the house where he rang the bell. The door was answered by a grey-haired lady with her hair drawn back in a bun. He stood talking to her for a few minutes and then when he returned to the car his face was even graver.

'He's not there,' he announced. 'His landlady tells me that he was in bed with the flu, but seemed to be getting better and he started going out. Yesterday afternoon, however, he packed up most of his things and drove off in his car saying he might not be back for some time. I know that he rang into the office yesterday and our secretary told him that I wanted to see him urgently regarding the estate of the late Mrs Fletcher.

'I agree that this does not look good for Mr Sergeant. If he is responsible then it seems as if he's realised that something has gone wrong with his plans and done a bunk.' Mr Drury's lapse into slang was a symptom of his growing agitation.

'I am afraid this is increasingly looking like a matter for the police. I would however like to make one further effort to trace him before taking such a dramatic step. You will appreciate that I have been in practice in this village nearly all my working life, and publicity attaching to a case like this would be severely detrimental to me. That would be so even if Mr Sergeant proved to have acted correctly – it will be very difficult to keep a secret in such a small village once it gets into the hands of the police.' Mr Drury slumped despairingly behind the steering wheel.

'Also, if and when we bring the police in, they will quite possibly wish to impound the clock and it may then be quite some time before the whole affair can be sorted out, particularly if Mr Sergeant cannot be found.

'Without prejudicing matters and strictly off the record, I would say your position looks the least comfortable, Mrs Campbell.' The poor lady's expression changed dramatically. Having been buoyed up by the discovery of the cheque, she was now once again facing the loss of her money.

'However, in the event of this whole affair turning out to be the fault of Mr Sergeant, and therefore of my practice, I can tell you that we carry professional indemnity insurance, although I would have to read the small print to make sure that a case like this was covered.'

'Well, I do hope so,' Mrs Campbell observed.

'I have to admit I don't know an awful lot about Mr Sergeant. He's quite a young man; I understand he comes from Edinburgh. He moved into digs that I helped him find when he joined the practice earlier this year. I expect I have an address for him in Edinburgh back in the office, and that may be the best clue to his whereabouts, but I suppose he's very unlikely to go back there now. I would have taken a reference at the time of engagement, but I doubt that would be of much help.'

Andrew joined in the conversation. 'The one good thing is that it looks as if it's only recently that he's realised that he may have been rumbled. So he may not yet have had time, or bothered, to dispose of the loot, so to speak.'

'But where do we start looking?' asked the bemused Mrs Campbell. Andrew took up the conversation again.

'Are we all agreed that we have a go at finding him before we tell the police, in the hope that we can retrieve the money before he disposes of it? Mrs Campbell can then have the money, Daphne has the clock and Mr Drury can take whatever action he likes to save his good name,' he said positively.

They looked round at themselves. They were an unlikely and ill-matched group. Mr Drury, a sixty-year-old solicitor, portly, avuncular, somewhat short of breath, unmarried and wearing his usual dark suit and tie. Seated next to him was Mrs Campbell, probably not quite so old and much more sprightly, single, leading a double life that involved selling antiques in a small Scottish village for a good part of the year, then departing to a warmer climate in the winter to live it up on the profits. In the back was Andrew, younger again, recently bereaved, much travelled and worldly-wise, but with little local knowledge beyond what he knew about his mother's cottage. Next to him was Daphne, also single, living at home with her mother and working at the Foreign Office. Practical and down-to-earth, possibly in a rut before receiving that fateful letter, and like her cousin, with very little local knowledge.

'Yes, I agree.' Each member of the entourage was quite firm in the undertaking.

'We'd better introduce ourselves more informally. I'm Andrew and this is my cousin Daphne.'

'I'm Mary,' said Mrs Campbell.

'And I'm George,' said Mr Drury.

'Right,' Andrew said, taking charge, 'I suggest that first we have a look at his rooms to see if there are any clues there – that might be a job for you, George, as you know the landlady. And then we can go to that pub we have just passed on the way here and discuss our options.'

'Very good,' George agreed, 'and I can telephone my secretary to tell her I won't be in this afternoon and to cancel my engagements. Here goes.' He once again levered his portly frame out of the small car and climbed the steep steps, already puffing by the time he reached the top. The landlady was soon at the door in response to his ring.

'Sorry to trouble you again, Mrs McDuff, but would you mind if I had a look round Mr Sergeant's rooms? I think he may have something I need.'

'Not at all, Mr Drury,' the landlady replied, anxious to please someone who had introduced her tenant. 'Do you think Mr Sergeant will be away long?'

'I don't know at this stage,' he replied cautiously. 'Can I further intrude on your hospitality and ask if my three clients in the car could also come in, as it's rather cold sitting out there and I don't know how long I should be?'

Again the landlady agreed readily and George Drury beckoned his new-found comrades to come in. Mr Sergeant had occupied the whole of the upper floor in the large house, comprising four rooms. After telling them the rooms were not locked, Mrs McDuff disappeared into a back room, while the four visitors climbed the stairs to the landing with George bringing up the rear, puffing. They decided that the best course of action, since there were four rooms and four people, was that each should take a room to search. It soon became apparent that their quarry had left very little behind to indicate where he had gone.

Daphne searched a room that looked like a study, full of books, many of them legal, and magazines. There was a computer screen on a table at one end, but the main power block of the computer was missing. Nor were there any discs or anything similar that might have information stored. There were no papers or documents. The drawers in a desk were devoid of anything that could have been of help.

Mary Campbell searched the lounge. Again there were quite a lot of books and magazines, but no diaries or address books or anything that had any writing on it that would have given any clues. The pictures on the walls looked as if they belonged to the landlady, being largely of sailing ships against Scottish backgrounds. And as in Daphne's room, there was nothing of interest in any of the drawers or cupboards.

Andrew took what was obviously the spare room. Its sole contents were a large number of empty cardboard boxes.

Somewhat forlornly he went through each box without finding anything of interest. One set of boxes had obviously contained the computer and its related equipment, but the rest of them were a nondescript lot.

George Drury went through the bedroom. Some clothes had been left behind. There were three suits hanging in the wardrobe, several ties, shirts and two pairs of smart black shoes. But once again, no papers or anything written.

After twenty minutes of fruitless searching they came together on the landing and decided to give up.

'Did you find what you were looking for?' the landlady enquired.

'I'm afraid not,' replied George Drury.

'I'm not surprised. He took three cases and a lot of stuff with him. There's not much left, is there?'

'No. I don't suppose he mentioned where he was going?'

'No, he never even said goodbye. He just loaded up his car and drove away. Is he coming back?'

'I hope so.'

They returned to the car and drove to the pub in silence. George made his phone call and they all sat round the table while they waited for the lunch they had ordered.

'Well, has anyone anything positive to report?' Andrew asked. 'The only things in my room were empty boxes.'

'I couldn't find anything of interest in the lounge,' admitted Mary. 'Just loads of books and magazines.'

'The same in the study,' added Daphne, 'plenty of legal books, but no travel guides, diaries or papers that might indicate where he was going.'

'I searched the bedroom,' said George. 'No useful papers or documents there either. He has left behind his business suits, shirts, ties and shoes – I suppose they were too bulky to pack.'

'So he's not going to take up a position in a rival solicitors then.' Andrew tried to lighten the sombre mood round the table.

'Or any other respectable job,' added Daphne.

'So therefore he's going somewhere away from his usual pattern of life, doing something that involves wearing casual clothes,' Mary's contribution was more constructive. 'What does he look like?'

'He's a very big man,' George told her, 'over six feet tall, large, but not particularly muscular, just large. He's aged about twenty-five, dark, wears glasses.'

'And Scottish?'

'Yes, that's right, strong accent.'

'I think I met him the day before yesterday. I called in at my neighbour's shop on my way back from Madeira to see if everything was all right next door. It was quite late and she was just closing up when a man of that description came in. He seemed in quite a hurry. My friend sells sweaters and woollen goods. He had a job finding a sweater his size. And he asked if she had any waterproof ones.'

At this apparently random piece of information they all became more alert.

'There were a lot of boating magazines in the study,' said Daphne.

'And in the lounge, which also had loads of pictures of sailing ships on the walls,' added Mary.

'And now I come to think of it, one of the empty boxes in the spare room was labelled oilskins,' contributed Andrew.

'And I can remember that boating and sailing were two of the interests he listed when he applied for the position with us,' George informed them. 'He often used to talk about boating and having a boat, but I'm pretty sure he didn't own one.'

'But he will soon,' Andrew said, 'I bet he's kitted himself to go off in a boat and the money will be used to buy it.'

At this point their lunches were served. They attacked the food with keen appetites now that they felt that they had a positive lead. Daphne turned to George and Mary. 'You're the two with local knowledge,' she said. 'He's in a hurry.

101

Where would someone go round here to find a boat?'

'There are two small fishing harbours on the coast, each of them about an hour's drive away,' George told her. 'Both once had a good trade, but the fishing industry has suffered badly in recent years. There are few working boats left. If it's a fishing boat he wants I imagine he won't have much difficulty finding one. They will be well pleased to sell their surplus vessels.'

'I doubt if he would go for a fishing boat,' said Mary. 'I've seen those boats. It's true they are not very big, but they would still need a crew. In his position he's likely to be on his own. Remember that it is probably only in the last day or two that he has realised he might be found out; up till then he would have thought he could carry on his job undetected and spend the money as he liked. Now he has got to make a quick getaway. So he'll need a power boat, not a sailing boat – if he really is going to try to escape on a boat it will be difficult enough in a power boat at this time of year, particularly if he has to do everything by himself. But that doesn't help in selecting which of the two harbours to go for first. They both have been changing the berths away from traditional fishing to provide for the wealthy pleasure-craft people.'

George peered out of the window. The weather had not changed. Everything outside was covered with an inch or more of snow. 'As I'm going to be driving I would prefer to go to Portham first. It's a better road for my poor wee car. If he is not there we can take the coast road round to the other harbour, Dunechurch.' Their plan of campaign agreed, they rapidly finished their meal and settled the bill.

'I suggest we all keep our coats on, as the heater in my car is not all that efficient,' George warned them. Daphne had brought her thick all-purpose overcoat she had bought in Rome with its belt secured by a heavy ornate buckle that she tightened as she went out into the falling snow. Andrew had one of his recently-purchased sweaters, but only a thin

102

anorak over that. 'You will have to keep me warm at the back, Daphne,' he said invitingly. Mary had a smart fawn three-quarter length coat with a hood which she pulled up to cover her hair. George Drury wore the standard black gent's overcoat that he had bought twenty years ago. The four of them squeezed into the car, George at the wheel, Mary beside him, with Daphne and Andrew together at the back. George engaged gear, grasping the steering wheel possessively, and peered through his glasses at the wall of snow that was now hitting the windscreen. They had already gone three miles before George plucked up enough courage to get into top gear. Daphne was itching to get behind the wheel – she had already made three journeys recently in similar conditions and felt she could make a better job of it than George, but didn't dare offer to drive. She remembered the attitude of the Croatian car hire owner both to women drivers and to someone else driving, so instead she snuggled up to Andrew who put his arm round her.

'I think, George, that you should lead the investigation, if and when we do catch up with our friend,' Andrew said. 'As you suggested earlier, he may have a logical explanation although that looks increasingly doubtful. And if he does try to pull the wool over our eyes you will be the best person to see through his cover.'

George agreed. 'I just hope we can resolve this without bringing in the police,' he said, 'but I agree this has all the appearance of being a complicated case of theft.'

11

Despite the slow speed at which they were travelling, nothing overtook them and hardly any cars passed in the opposite direction. While for George in the driving seat the conditions were a nightmare, for the three passengers the countryside through which they travelled was a delight. 'This is as near a Christmas card picture as I have seen,' Daphne enthused. 'Croatia wasn't as pretty as this.' It was a full hour before a sign loomed up through the snow advising them they had arrived at Portham. They drove down to the water's edge where a variety of small vessels were bobbing up and down in the protected waters of the miniature harbour.

Absolutely nothing seemed to be happening anywhere. All the boats were at anchor, none was moving and there was nobody about on any of them to suggest that anything would happen in the near future. Neither did there seem to be any activity on the quayside. There were no shops in the harbour area, just a few nondescript stone-built structures that had seen better times, but now looked largely derelict. The only sign of life came from a long single storey shed-like building at the further end of the quayside, where a thick plume of smoke emerged from the top of a long metal chimney and battled against the snow, while a beam of light shafted out of the only window facing them.

They pulled up opposite this ramshackle building that looked as if it was the centre of the local fishing trade. Outside were lobster pots, empty wooden crates, gas cylinders and an upturned rowing boat that would never put to sea again. A name was painted in large letters along the length of the building, but the paintwork had peeled to such an extent that it was no longer possible to make out what the name was.

'It doesn't look as if anyone is making a quick getaway here,' observed Daphne, alluding to Mary's earlier remark. 'In fact, if I were thinking about making a quick getaway this is about the last place I would choose.'

'You haven't seen Dunechurch yet,' replied Mary.

'I suppose it was a pretty long shot to think he would try to make off in a boat. Pure theory. We can't even be sure he's not going to turn up at the office next week.' George had never been an optimist and recent events had combined with the weather to bring out his natural pessimism.

'Anyway, let's go in this place over there and ask. We've come so far we might as well make some enquiries. Are you coming with me, Andrew?' Daphne asked.

Andrew agreed and got out of the car with the two women while George remained behind. 'That drive was a bit of a strain,' he confessed, 'I'll rest here while you see what you can find out in there, but give me a call if you need me.'

The snow had eased up, and the influence of the sea was now melting it as it fell. They walked across to the decrepit building and pushed open the door. It was immediately obvious where the maritime population of Portham had disappeared to – they were all inside this building. It was packed with men dressed in thick woollen sweaters and oilskins. The newcomers were assailed by the smells of wet wool, fish and smoke from the stove at the end of the room. The only woman among them was standing behind a small counter at the far end serving tea and cakes. All the men were seated.

An instant silence descended as the three squeezed in and Andrew endeavoured to shut the door behind him.

Daphne was the first to recover her composure.

'Good afternoon,' she said. All eyes were fixed on her but no one replied. 'We were wondering whether this was the sort of place where a boat could be bought or hired?' she enquired hesitantly.

'What sort of boat are ye looking for?' one of the younger men seated nearest her asked.

'It would be a power boat not a fishing boat. A small one, that one person could sail by himself.'

'We're all fishing folk here. We could take you out on a short trip if you wished, but it hardly seems the weather for it. Were you thinking of today?'

Daphne's hopes of finding out anything useful were receding rapidly. 'Well, it wasn't for me actually.' Her London accent seemed very out of place in the close confines of the fishermen's hut.

'You could buy my boat,' volunteered an old bearded gentleman at the back of the room, 'and me with it.' This produced guffaws of laughter from the seated audience.

A third voice spoke up from the back. 'There are sailing trips organised from here, but not at this time of the year. If it's pleasure craft you're looking for, you need to come back in the summer. That's when most of the people who own the pleasure boats you see out there are about. There are a few boat owners who come down here on winter weekends to clean their boats, but not on a day like this. It's only us fishermen who work in this weather.' The fisherman took a swig out of his mug of tea.

Daphne felt like asking him what they were all doing inside if they were such keen workers, but knew that would not be diplomatic. Instead she said, 'Thank you for your time. We are sorry to intrude. I realise now this is not the right place to get a pleasure craft.'

106

The lady at the back asked if she would like a cup of tea, but Daphne declined. 'We must get going,' she said, as Andrew and Mary made to go out.

'It's a funny thing, but you're the second person who's been in here today asking to buy a boat. Are you connected?' the tea lady asked.

The three immediately stopped in their tracks. 'We are looking for a boat in connection with someone else.' Daphne chose her words carefully. 'What did this other person look like?'

'A very tall, large man, dark, with glasses, not a sassenach.'

'That sounds very like the person we are connected with.'

'Well, he was very keen to buy a vessel just as you have described, and he was in a hurry too. But as you have learned, we don't have anything like that for sale as far as we know. As you see, we are all fisher folk in here.'

'Did you say he came here earlier today?'

'Yes, around ten o'clock this morning, and like you he didn't want to stop for a cup of tea.'

Inspired by this news, Daphne thanked the tea lady, and the three of them turned to leave again when the lady fired a parting shot. 'I told him to go to Dunechurch, there's a chandlers there, they usually have details of any boats that are for sale in this part of the world and act for the owners in any sale. Why don't you go there, it's only about half an hour on the coast road.'

Daphne thanked her for the third time and said she certainly would take her advice. Then all three emerged into the fresh air, relieved to be out of the overwhelming atmosphere inside, and well pleased with this latest piece of information. Back in the car, they gave George the news. 'At last we've got something positive,' he said, perking up, engaging gear and driving off.

The coast road followed the inlets of the sea, but was generally level, while the snow had stopped falling and the road was not icy, so George was able to make good progress. 'We've still got another two hours of daylight,' he said hopefully. 'Things look a bit more encouraging now. I can't believe John Sergeant would have been able to find and buy a boat all in one day, and then have time to sail off.'

Before long they reached the outskirts of the small fishing port and drove down to the harbour. Although the terrain round the harbour was nowhere near as rugged as at Portham and, with the wintry sun trying to break out, it looked generally less bleak, in one respect it was very similar – the whole place looked totally deserted. The harbour itself was divided into two parts by a stone jetty that looked as if it had been recently built. It was in the shape of a dog's leg with a bend to the right which created a very small marina. A dozen or more small pleasure craft were berthed in the lee of the marina, while a handful of fishing vessels were moored on the left of the jetty. There was a line of buildings facing the marina, all stone-built, but now, with the afternoon drawing on, some were at least showing lights at the windows. The first had a sign, 'locally caught fish lobster and crab', underneath which hung a much smaller sign which read 'Closed'. Then came a series of uneven buildings that seemed to be workshops, stores and even one or two houses, but none was open for business. The very last building in the line bore the sign 'Yacht Chandlers' followed by a list of the various marine items that were on offer. Lights shone out of the windows.

'That must be the place,' said Mary, 'and it even looks as if it is open.' George pulled up outside the chandlers and they all got out.

'I'll come with you this time,' he said, 'I feel like stretching my legs.' He had all of ten yards to walk to the front door of the chandlers.

'Well, I'm going to stretch my legs round the harbour,' Daphne said. 'It doesn't need four of us to ask questions. I did most of the talking last time, and it was really fuggy in there then. I don't fancy another session like that. I really felt out of place among all those fishermen.'

The three of them trooped into the chandlers leaving Daphne to take her walk outside. Once inside, they discovered a quite different set-up from the fishermen's hut at Portham. Down one side was a counter where all the yachting and fishing gear was obviously sold. The counter was cluttered with a variety of different sailing apparatus among which pots of paint and varnish figured prominently. An open door in the wall behind the counter led to a store-room at the back. There was no one behind the counter, but four men were seated on chairs spread out in the fairly large space on the public side of the counter. They were all drinking mugs of tea, but turned to greet their visitors in an amiable way. Three were dressed in the usual thick sweaters and rugged trousers, but one wore a suit. He stood up and pleasantly remarked on how bad the weather had been, how it was now clearing up and how much better the forecast for tomorrow was. He then went on to describe what the weather had been like over the past week and how difficult it was for anyone who had to go out in it. In fact, weather was obviously a matter of supreme interest to him. Moreover, he was clearly delighted to have a fresh audience to regale with his favourite topic. He was now in full flight, branching out into the weather conditions in the North Sea generally, when Andrew decided he ought to interrupt if he was ever going to get anywhere.

'I realise that this is not really the sort of day to be talking about it, but we have really come to enquire about a boat. I wonder...' Andrew got no further when the weather enthusiast interrupted in turn.

'A boat! Do come into my office.' So saying, he led the visitors into a small room at the further end of the chandlery, and found them chairs to sit on. This is going to be a long session, thought Andrew, if what he can find to say about the weather is anything to go by. Sure enough, the young suited gentleman set off on another long dissertation on a subject that seemed as dear to his heart as the weather, without really revealing much beyond the fact that the chandlery was agent in a variety of ways for boat owners, boat hirers and boat insurers. In fact, he seemed remarkably indifferent as to why Andrew should have come to his office. It took an interminable time before Andrew could get him to home in on what he wanted.

'Yes, we do have some boat owners who might be prepared to sell or even hire,' he finally admitted. There followed long descriptions of several boats which were moored in the marina and of others further afield, supported by photographs and printed details of the vessels. None of these was likely to be appropriate, being generally too large and too expensive. Andrew was about to ask whether anyone else had been in today looking for a boat, which was after all the purpose of their visit, when the young man announced he would get them all some tea, and disappeared out of the door.

'Oh dear,' said Mary, 'and I thought it was women who were supposed to do all the talking.' They sat patiently waiting their host's return, with only the pictures of boats adorning the walls to relieve their bored anxiety. 'Daphne will have explored the whole of Dunechurch at this rate,' Andrew remarked.

The young man returned with mugs of tea and a bowl of dubious-looking sugar, informing them that they could call him Donald. He was about to continue his description of the various boats that were on offer when Andrew decided to bring matters to a head.

'We are in fact looking for a boat in conjunction with someone else,' he said, 'In order not to waste your time can I first ask you whether you have had anyone else in here today asking about a vessel?'

'Yes, I have,' replied Donald with surprising brevity.

'A tall large man, probably local, with glasses?'

'Yes, I have indeed been dealing with such a man.'

'The man's name is Mr John Sergeant.'

'Is he a friend of yours?'

'He is my partner,' interrupted George, 'I am a solicitor.'

'Ah, that's interesting. Well, we have now arranged something for Mr Sergeant. We do have boats for sale here, but he was in rather a hurry. I couldn't immediately contact the owner of the one that most suited him, and, er, some of these vessels are in a moderately high price bracket, although nothing like you might find in the South of France. I agreed to allow Mr Sergeant to hire the boat for a while as a means of trying it out. He left a cheque to cover the cost of the hire and to act as a deposit in the event of a purchase.

'I said he could go on the boat today and have arranged to put some diesel in it. Although it's quite small it has a powerful enough engine and is equipped with an automatic pilot that's been installed fairly recently. He was quite keen to find a craft that he could sail by himself. The boat itself was built quite a long time ago to the specifications of its original owner, which wouldn't suit everybody – hence the very fair price. He seemed quite happy when I showed him over the craft before lunch and he has been out there ever since. I did advise him that it would be unwise to go out in this weather, although I see it has stopped snowing and the wind has now dropped. He seems fairly knowledgeable, your partner, will you be going with him?'

Without really waiting for an answer, Donald moved over to the window which had misted up as a result of so many bodies in the small space. With the sleeve of his suit he wiped an area clear and peered out across the marina.

'Ah,' he said, his lower jaw remaining open...

111

12

Meanwhile Daphne decided to take a brisk walk along the short marina jetty to look at the boats tied up against the protective wall. It had stopped snowing and the weak December sun was doing its best to brighten up the rather sombre granite stonework. She buckled her thick Italian overcoat around her and picked her way carefully along the jetty, avoiding the ropes, stanchions and other obstacles that threatened to trip her up and send her into the freezing waters below. She came to the end of the jetty, drawing level with the last of the moored boats. It was the smallest in the line, with a neat enclosed cockpit above a short ladder leading to a tiny cabin below. Daphne stood there for a few minutes breathing in the fresh sea air, when she became aware of a movement on the boat.

A head appeared out of the open window of the cockpit. 'It's Miss Fleet, isn't it? The lady who inherited a clock. What in the world are you doing here?' The 'r' in world was firmly pronounced. Daphne had no doubt who it was addressing her – John Sergeant, the man they were looking for.

'Why, Mr Sergeant,' she said nervously. Having found her quarry unexpectedly, she was at a loss as to what she should do next. Mr Sergeant opened the door to the cockpit and squeezed his bulky frame out onto the deck of the boat which was some way below the level of the jetty. A set of slimy, seaweed-covered steps led down to where the boat was moored.

'Come aboard and you can tell me what you think of this wee craft.' Seeing Daphne hesitate, he clambered out onto the steps and offered her his hand. Automatically she took the proferred hand and allowed herself to be helped onto the boat.

'There's not a lot of room, is there?' he volunteered. 'I'm thinking of buying it and have hired it for a wee while to see how it handles. Come inside and I'll make you a cup of tea.' He ushered Daphne down the few steps that led to the cabin below and opened the door. Even Daphne had to crouch to get in; for John Sergeant the lack of space was even more acute. A small narrow table occupied the centre of the cabin, with an equally narrow bench on either side. At the further end there was a small sink and the absolute minimum of cooking facilities.

'I haven't yet managed the kitchen but I do have a flask of tea that was made only a short while ago on land,' John Sergeant told her. 'I'll pour you a cup. Do you take sugar?' When Daphne said that she did, it took Mr Sergeant quite a while before he could locate a tin marked 'sugar'. It proved to be empty. 'Never mind,' said Daphne, 'I'll drink it as it comes.'

The two sat facing each other across the narrow table as they sipped their tea. John Sergeant now looked even bigger in the confined space than she remembered from their previous encounter in the solicitor's office. He was wearing a bulky sweater that she recognised as having come from the woollen shop. He fidgetted with his mug of tea as he described the boat they were in. 'It's got a good engine that they tell me has been recently overhauled. It will go quite a distance before it needs refuelling. I've done a bit of sailing in the last few years, but this will be the first boat I have ever actually owned if I decide to buy it. I haven't made up my mind yet. I'm not sure if I can cope with this very small cabin down here. And I have yet to give it a run although I did start the engine earlier. It makes a bonny roar.' For the first time a smile flitted across the big man's dour countenance. 'Are you interested in boats, Miss Fleet? Is that why you're here in this out of the way place? If I remember rightly, you are a Londoner?'

Daphne did not know how to answer his question. Had the four of them been together it would have been a straightforward case of getting him to admit what he was up to. She knew that at least George ought to be with her in case Mr Sergeant was able to offer some technical reason as to why he was not in his office and what he had done with the clock. Also, she was not really sure whether the man facing her knew that he had been 'rumbled' as Andrew put it, assuming of course that he was indeed guilty. Certainly he gave no sign that he had been found out.

Daphne hesitated. She felt she could not ask him outright what he had done with her clock without some introductory explanation of how she knew that things were not right. If she voiced her suspicions now and he denied everything, what could she do? How stupid to have got into this situation! Why on earth had she come aboard this wretched little boat instead of waiting for the others? Seeing her hesitate, Mr Sergeant offered her a way out.

'Perhaps you've come back to Scotland to see your aunt's cottage again before it's sold?' he suggested. For once Daphne decided that lying was the only course open to her and nodded in agreement, although she realised that this was a pretty flimsy reason for being there. 'And now you are doing the rounds of the local sights. I remember when I first saw you, you asked about our local attractions, but in the event you did not spend too much time visiting on that occasion. Now you are making up for your earlier lack of interest?'

114

Mr Sergeant eyed her speculatively across the table. Daphne felt that judgement was now being passed on her. The tables had somehow been turned, with the roles of the two participants reversed. She should be asking the questions, not agreeing to made-up answers.

The big man picked up his mug and drained the remainder of his tea. 'I've always wanted a boat, you know, Miss Fleet. I've often gone out crewing on other people's boats, but that's never the same as having your own craft. This one may not be the biggest vessel in the world, but it should do me, I think. It's an opportunity I don't want to pass up. I want you to know how important it is to me and how much I should be disappointed if I were unable to have it.'

Daphne said nothing as she was not sure what to make of the solicitor's remarks. She was increasingly certain that he must know why she was here. He carried on, almost as if he was talking to himself.

'I've executed a number of wills. The beneficiaries often didn't know what they were going to receive, they scarcely knew the deceased either. If it was money, they spent immediately what their elderly relatives had taken a lifetime to accumulate. If it was some valuable heirloom that had been in their family for generations, they sold it for as much as they could get and then spent the proceeds. I've been asked to amend trusts set up to prevent estates being dissipated by greedy survivors. I've been asked to alter wills after death so that relatives could get their hands on the money quickly. It doesn't seem fair really. If I were Chancellor of the Exchequer I'd tax inheritances as hard as I could.' He sounded very bitter, and his face had resumed its usual lugubrious appearance. Daphne was becoming increasingly nervous. She wanted to let him know that she was not alone, but knew she could not tell him that George and Mary were here because he would then definitely realise that they knew what he was up to.

'My cousin will be waiting for me on the shore. I told him I was just going for a short walk and would not be long,' Daphne told him without much conviction.

'You found your cousin then? He will have told you about your inheritance.' He paused. 'It's getting cold in here. I'll start up the engine and the heating will come on.' Ignoring Daphne's remarks, he got up, opened the door, and disappeared up the steps, closing the door behind him. Daphne heard him in the cockpit above. Then the engine came alive with a roar. She got up and tried the door. It was locked! It had a Yale lock which locked automatically on shutting.

She heard him moving about on the deck above. What was he doing up there? She looked out of the small porthole of the cabin. The boat was moving! As she watched, the jetty steadily disappeared out of her vision. She banged on the door and then on the ceiling to no avail. Desperately she cried out, but she knew that it was unlikely that anyone else would be around to hear her cries. She banged on the door again, first with her fists and then with her feet. It did not seem all that strong and the lock was only a Yale. She looked about her. In one corner of the cabin was a length of heavy wood, splintered at one end as if it had been broken off. She picked it up and used it as a battering ram against the flimsy Yale lock. After four thudding blows the Yale gave way and the door flew open.

Keeping the length of wood in her hand she moved cautiously up the steps. What was he intending to do? The boat was now a good hundred yards from the end of the jetty and picking up speed. As she climbed up the steps she could see the rapidly receding harbour. A group of people were running out of the chandlery. She emerged on to the deck, the wind created by the speeding boat catching her breath, and moved to the stern where she waved frantically to the figures that were now running along the jetty. Already they were too far away to be able to understand her shouted calls for help.

The engine was running at full throttle making the whole boat vibrate. She turned to face the bow of the vessel. John Sergeant was inside the cockpit and did not appear to realise she was behind him on the stern of the deck. Should she try to rush him and take him by surprise? What was he going to do with her anyway? While she stood there wondering uncertainly what to do he turned his head and saw her on the deck. He switched to automatic pilot, came out of the cockpit and down the port side towards her. She backed away to the opposite side until she felt the metal guard rail in her back.

'Don't come any closer!' she warned him and raised the heavy piece of wood she was still holding.

'Give me that,' he said moving closer towards her and raising his hand. Daphne thrust the piece of wood at his stomach, but it was too heavy to wield effectively as a weapon. He caught hold of the other end, pulling her towards him. Although Daphne was fit and strong, she was no match for the younger sixteen-stone man, who forced her back against the railing. He wrenched the piece of wood out of her hands. She groaned as his heavy weight squeezed her hard back on the single guard rail.

Suddenly there was a loud crack as the metal railing snapped. Daphne felt herself falling backwards over the stern of the boat with the big man on top of her. As she fell, the broken end of the rail caught in the belt of her Italian overcoat and she was swung out and then backwards over the side of the fast-moving boat as the broken rail bent back on itself under the weight of the bodies. The big man hit the water below her with a tremendous splash and then disappeared from sight below the waves. She was left suspended by the belt of her coat over the side of the boat, her feet already in the cold sea, and her back to the side of the boat. Somehow she reached out and caught hold of the upright stanchion above her, first with one hand only, and then twisting round, with both hands. But her belt was still caught on

117

the broken rail at the back. Letting go with one hand she desperately unbuckled the belt. Then, restoring her grip with both hands, she summoned up all her strength to pull herself back on the deck, leaving her life-saving belt still hanging on the broken rail. 'I'm not losing that – it saved my life,' she said as she reached down the side of the boat to retrieve it.

The boat was still moving away from the harbour under the automatic pilot. The wake was a straight line of foam in the middle of which a head bobbed up and down. So John Sergeant was still alive. An arm waved forlornly at the boat, which was already too far away for Daphne to hear any cries for help. She decided she had better do something and shakily made her way to the cockpit. The controls did not look all that complex. The automatic pilot was clearly labelled. She switched back to manual. Next she located the throttle and reduced speed. Now she was in a position to turn the boat round. Taking a firm grip of the wheel she made a slow turn until she was facing the shore. She was surprised at how far out she was, but saw that in the distance one of the fishing boats was making out from the jetty. But what she was not able to do was to retrace exactly the outward path of the boat. John Sergeant was nowhere to be seen. It had taken her perhaps twenty minutes to get back on board the boat, master the controls and bring it back to where she thought he had gone overboard. Even if he were a good swimmer, could he last that long in the North Sea in December? Daphne slowed the engine at the same time following a zig-zag course, but all in vain. He was nowhere to be seen. She made a complete turn in the area where she thought the incident had taken place without finding a trace of the unfortunate solicitor.

After a short while the fishing boat from the harbour arrived on the scene. Daphne shouted a brief explanation of what had happened and both boats circled the area without success. In the end they gave up and made their way back to the marina. With the help of the crew of the fishing boat and all the people who had by now assembled on the jetty the boat was moored. Daphne climbed ashore exhausted. The first to greet her was Andrew. 'Thank God you are safe,' he said, embracing her fervently. Putting his arm round her shoulder he helped her back to the chandlers where as many people as possible squeezed in to learn what had happened. It was a long time since the inhabitants of Dunechurch had had such excitement.

After Daphne had taken off her sodden Italian overcoat that had played such an important part in her life since she bought it, she recounted the drama aboard the boat. 'I don't really know what he hoped to do with me, but he was certainly keen to have the boat. The strange thing is that he never admitted to taking the clock or doing anything wrong, but he was a very embittered man. I think he had almost certainly realised that I knew he had given me the wrong clock, but I can't be even certain of that. Now we shall never know.'

'It took us some time to find out that John Sergeant was here,' Andrew told her, 'and when we did the boat was already under way. Fortunately, with Donald's encouragement, it didn't take too long to persuade a fishing crew to go out. As far as we could see from a distance he was trying to kidnap you.'

The local policeman was one of the people who had crowded into the chandlery. He and Daphne were shown into Donald's office where she gave him a simple but exact account of events without offering any explanation as to why they took place. Ominously the policeman asked Daphne if she would give a more complete statement later that day when she would be more composed.

Then George had a long chat with Donald, using his legal expertise to extract the maximum benefit from the situation. The cheque that John Sergeant had left could not be presented, but it did tell George where his former partner had banked the money from the sale of the clock. George was confident that eventually he would be able to return the money to the estate, without, he hoped, having to bring in the police.

Daphne's clothes were still wet and she felt physically exhausted from her experience on the boat. She was dying for a hot bath and a chance to relax. They learnt that Dunechurch had only one pub, but it did offer bed and breakfast accommodation. They extracted themselves from the throng in the chandlers and George drove them the short distance round to the pub, the White Hart.

'It's getting late,' he said, 'I don't fancy driving back in the dark even if it has stopped snowing. If the rest of you agree, I suggest we see if we can spend the night here. We can then go back to Cruff in the morning.' Andrew agreed readily, Mary said she would do whatever George preferred, but Daphne was hoping to change her wet clothes back in the hotel in Cruff, although she wanted a bath as soon as possible.

When they arrived at the White Hart, they discovered there was something of a problem – only three rooms were available. This led to some very delicate discussions with the men preferring to stay while the women were now wanting to drive back to Cruff. The landlady helped to tilt the scales in favour of the men when she said she thought she could find a clean change of clothes for Daphne. Finally, and not too reluctantly, Daphne allowed herself to be persuaded to share a room having two single beds and a bath with Andrew. 'After all,' he said, 'I did put you to bed in Croatia. You didn't complain then.'

Daphne went upstairs to luxuriate in a well-deserved hot bath. Mary too took a bath, but the two men settled down in front of an open fire with a whisky while Andrew described some of his more adventurous assignments to George who listened with interest. 'I don't think that's a life I would have been cut out for,' he confessed, 'glamorous though it sounds.

120

My father was a solicitor. I never thought to be anything else. In my own little pond in Cruff I'm quite an important fish. But as the years go by I find myself looking back not forwards. Now I've reached a certain age I do think I might have missed out in my youth.' George grew philosophical over his whisky.

Andrew also became introspective. 'I've always wanted to travel. My job gives me a sense of satisfaction, but the pay is poor. I live in rented digs in Rome which is an exciting city, but also an expensive one. I don't own a house and I haven't saved a bean. I'm starting to wonder whether I shouldn't use my modest inheritance to change my lifestyle, buy a house and quit all this dangerous gadding about while I'm still in one piece, although what I should do for a living I've no idea. I have few qualifications, beyond an ability to exchange a few words in about twenty different languages. Perhaps I should have a chat with Daphne. She has travelled, but at least she has a career and a proper home to come back to in the evenings.'

The landlady had found Daphne a change of clothes. She couldn't relax after all, her mind was still going over the day's events, so she went downstairs to join the others at dinner. The landlady had cooked an excellent casserole of local beef which they accompanied with a couple of bottles of red wine.

Andrew resumed his self-assessment. 'Daphne, I'm beginning to tire of my wandering lifestyle. Do you think I should give it all up and come back to England? You seem content with your lot.'

'You will find it rather boring, I think,' Daphne told him. 'And will you be content with us English girls after mixing with so many different exotic women from around the world?'

'I would be very content if they were like you, Daphne. You're all a man could wish for.'

Daphne felt her cheeks reddening. 'Coming from you, Andrew, that is indeed a compliment.'

Andrew made more complimentary remarks to Daphne during dinner. She felt on a high, the excitement of the day, the wine at the dinner table, Andrew's growing interest in her all serving to keep her pulse racing.

After dinner they were settling down in front of the fire with a liberal supply of whisky when the local policeman returned, this time accompanied by a woman police officer who carried the rank of sergeant. They asked Daphne if she would make a written statement about the day's events and if she would answer a few questions. Daphne in turn asked if the others could be present, and when this was agreed, they all sat down together.

Daphne then recounted the events on the boat while the policeman laboriously wrote them down. When she had finished she was asked to sign the notes. The police sergeant then asked if she would clarify a few points.

'Did you know Mr John Sergeant?' she asked.

'I met him briefly for the first time two or three weeks ago in his office in connection with my aunt's will,' Daphne replied a little nervously. 'He was not my solicitor.'

'Did he invite you on the boat?'

'Yes, he did.'

'And did you go of your own free will?'

'Yes, I did.'

'Did he make any suggestions to you while you were in the cabin?'

'No, he didn't.'

'Or make any improper advances?'

'No.'

'The door was locked with a Yale lock. Could it have locked by accident or by simply shutting the door?'

'Yes, that is possible.'

'Did he say he was going to leave the jetty or to sail off?'

'No, he didn't.'

'Were you surprised when that happened?'

'Yes, I was.'

'And you have no idea where he was going to take you?'

'None at all.'

'Or what he was going to do with you?'

'Again, no.' Daphne was beginning to feel on the defensive. It this went on much longer she would have to tell the police sergeant about the clock.

'One last question. The struggle on the deck. Do you think John Sergeant was trying to force you overboard – did he say anything to you?'

'He asked for the piece of wood I was holding, but I don't think he intended to push me over. It wouldn't have happened if the guard rail hadn't snapped and pitched us both over. I was just very lucky my belt got caught.'

'I see. I know from other witnesses that you made every effort to locate Mr Sergeant after he had fallen in the sea. I must ask you for your permanent address, and I think it quite possible you will be called upon again in the event of there being an inquest. We have yet to recover the body.'

She thanked Daphne and the two police officers took their leave.

'I've got a feeling I haven't heard the last of this,' Daphne said.

'If there is any problem over Mr Sergeant's part in all this, I will come forward with an explanation of what he had been doing with the will,' George told Daphne. 'For the time being I will concentrate on getting the money out of the bank where he has deposited it. I think this is as clear a case of money-laundering as one could find, and I don't anticipate any trouble. I hope to be able to exchange the money for the clock you are holding, Mary, then finally Daphne can have what is rightfully hers.'

They all raised their glasses to a successful outcome, then

repeated the toast several times until they all felt ready to retire.

George and Mary went up to their separate rooms while Daphne and Andrew went together to their shared room. The pub was quite old. The room was comparatively large with a high ceiling, one long window looking out to sea. A separate bathroom and toilet ocupied the remainder of the accommodation. The beds looked comfortable enough, but the most dominant feature of the room was an enormous wardrobe with full length doors each holding an inset mirror. Although it took up a great deal of space, the reflecting mirrors gave the room an appearance of endless depth.

Daphne went into the bathroom to repair as best she could the damage to her looks that the day's adventures had caused. She had no make-up, only a hairbrush that the landlady had provided and the minimal soap and towels always found in hotel bathrooms. She took off the clothes the landlady had given her, but kept on her underwear. Despite all that had happened to her during the day she no longer felt in the least bit tired. On the contrary, the after-effects of the action on the boat, together with Andrew's close presence, were now stimulating her. She felt in a highly charged state of mind. When she looked in the mirror she saw her face was glowing. 'How much of that is fresh air and how much is whisky?' She asked herself 'Anyway I'm going to bed like this.' She returned to the main room.

Andrew had also stripped to his pants and was sitting on one of the beds in front of the mirrors. Boldly, Daphne sat beside him. They looked at themselves in the giant mirrors. It was obvious they had common ancestors. Fair-haired, freckle-faced, snub-nosed, their features were so similar they could have been brother and sister. Their bodies, too, were matching, slim yet well built, both with long legs.

Their eyes met in the mirrors. Daphne watched in the mirror as Andrew put his arm round her shoulder and brought her to him. Their lips devoured each other's hungrily. The two bodies, matching in every way as if they had always been made for each other since birth, entwined incestuously. The two cousins were about to become something more . ᴇ.